GALDONI

Book 1

By Cheree L. Alsop

ISBN
Cover Design by Andy Hair
www.ChereeAlsop.com

PRAISE FOR CHEREE ALSOP

Galdoni

"I was pleasantly surprised by this book! The characters were so well written as if the words themselves became life. The sweet romance between hero and heroine made me root for the underdog more than I usually do! I definitely recommend this book!"

—Sara Phillipp

"Can't wait for the next book!! Original idea and great characters. Could not put the book down; read it in one sitting."

—StanlyDoo- Amazon Reviewer

"5 stars! Amazing read. The story was great- the plot flowed and kept throwing the unexpected at you. Wonderfully established setting in place; great character development, shown very well thru well placed dialogue- which in turn kept the story moving right along! No bog downs or boring parts in this book! Loved the originality that stemmed from ancient mysticism- bringing age old fiction into modern day reality. Recommend for teenage and older- action violence a little intense for preteen years, but overall this is a great action thriller slash mini romance novel."

—That Lisa Girl, Amazon Reviewer

The Silver Series

"Cheree Alsop has written *Silver* for the YA reader who enjoys both werewolves and coming-of-age tales. Although I don't fall into this demographic, I still found it an entertaining read on a long plane trip! The author has put a great deal of thought into balancing a tale that could apply to any teen (death of a parent, new school, trying to find one's place in the world) with the added spice of a youngster dealing with being exceptionally different from those around him, and knowing that puts him in danger."

—Robin Hobb, author of the Farseer Trilogy

"I honestly am amazed this isn't absolutely EVERYWHERE! Amazing book. Could NOT put it down! After reading this book, I purchased the entire series!"

—Josephine, Amazon Reviewer

"Great book, Cheree Alsop! The best of this kind I have read in a long time. I just hope there is more like this one."

—Tony Olsen

"I couldn't put the book down. I fell in love with the characters and how wonderfully they were written. Can't wait to read the 2nd!"

—Mary A. F. Hamilton

"A page-turner that kept me wide awake and wanting more. Great characters, well written, tenderly developed, and thrilling. I loved this book, and you will too."

—Valerie McGilvrey

Keeper of the Wolves

"This is without a doubt the VERY BEST paranormal romance/adventure I have ever read and I've been reading these types of books for over 45 years. Excellent plot, wonderful protagonists—even the evil villains were great. I read this in one sitting on a Saturday morning when there were so many other things I should have been doing. I COULD NOT put it down! I also appreciated the author's research and insights into the behavior of wolf packs. I will CERTAINLY read more by this author and put her on my 'favorites' list."

—N. Darisse

"This is a novel that will emotionally cripple you. Be sure to keep a box of tissues by your side. You will laugh, you will cry, and you will fall in love with Keeper. If you loved *Black Beauty* as a child, then you will truly love *Keeper of the Wolves* as an adult. Put this on your 'must read' list."

—Fortune Ringquist

"Cheree Alsop mastered the mind of a wolf and wrote the most amazing story I've read this year. Once I started, I couldn't stop reading. Personal needs no longer existed. I turned the last page with tears streaming down my face."

—Rachel Andersen, Amazon Reviewer

Thief Prince

"This book was a roller coaster of emotions: tears, laughter, anger, and happiness. I absolutely fell in love with all of the characters placed throughout this story. This author knows how to paint a picture with words."

—Kathleen Vales

"Awesome book! It was so action packed, I could not put it down, and it left me wanting more! It was very well written, leaving me feeling like I had a connection with the characters."

—M. A., Amazon Reviewer

"I am a Cheree Alsop junkie and I have to admit, hands down, this is my FAVORITE of anything she has published. In a world separated by race, fear and power are forced to collide in order to save them all. Who better to free them of the prejudice than the loyal heart of a Duskie? Adventure, incredible amounts of imagination, and description go into this world! It is a 'buy now and don't leave the couch until the last chapter has reached an end' kind of read!"

—Malcay, Amazon Reviewer

Small Town Superhero

"Anyone who grew up in a small town or around motorcycles will love this! It has great characters and flows well with martial arts fighting and conflicts involved."

—Karen, Amazon Reviewer

"Cheree Alsop has written a great book for youth and adults alike. . . *Small Town Superhero* had me from the first sentence through the end. I felt every sorrow, every pain, and the delight of rushing through the dark on a motorcycle. Descriptions in *Small Town Superhero* are so well written the reader is immersed in the town and lives of its inhabitants."

—Rachel Andersen, Amazon Reviewer

CHEREE ALSOP

Stolen

"This book will take your heart, make it a little bit bigger, and then fill it with love. I would recommend this book to anyone from 10-100. To put this book in words is like trying to describe love. I had just gotten it and I finished it the next day because I couldn't put it down. If you like action, thrilling fights, and/or romance, then this is the perfect book for you."

—Steven L. Jagerhorn

Heart of the Wolf

"This book is a roller coaster of emotions that will leave you exhausted!!! A beautiful fantasy filled with action and love. I recommend this book to all fantasy lovers and those who enjoy a heartbreaking love story that rivals that of Romeo and Juliet. I couldn't put this book down!"

—Amy May

ALSO BY CHEREE ALSOP

The Silver Series
Silver
Black
Crimson
Violet
Azure
Hunter
Silver Moon

The Small Town Superheroes Series
(Being published through Stonehouse Ink)
Small Town Superhero
The Small Town Superheroes
The Last Small Town Superhero

Galdoni
Heart of the Wolf
Keeper of the Wolves
Stolen
The Million Dollar Gift
Thief Prince
Shadows
Mist

To my husband, Michael Alsop.
Thank you for believing in me,
And for giving Kale his wings.

To my family for their support,
And for reading each copy.

I love you!

Chapter One

Free. The word burned in my mind. Above, Galdoni flew in pairs and trios past the sky-rise buildings. I fought back the urge to fly with them; it was better to have the stable ground under my feet after the world had just turned on end.

I flexed my wings, then tucked them tight against my back so they would be less obvious to the casual observer. A mob of humans bearing signs ringed the main gate through which most of the Galdoni left; luckily, it was publicity they sought and none of the protesters bothered with the few smaller gates like the one I used.

I looked back at the gray stone building in which I had lived my entire life. I felt a dull taint of fear and pushed it away, surprised that the emotion had survived my training. I gritted my teeth and stepped into the alley.

The fading sunlight didn't reach the shadows that clung to the walls and refuse. I stepped around an overflowing garbage bin. The scurry of tiny claws sounded against the cement; bigger footsteps echoed it, and a tiny shriek choked off to leave the air a bit colder.

As I made my way through the debris-littered darkness, I began to second-guess my decision to walk, but there wasn't enough room to spread my wings between the claustrophobic walls. A rusted fire escape hung crookedly down the side of one condemned building. I set a foot on the bottom rung with the thought of climbing to the top of the building so I could fly. I had just put my weight on the rung when a yell came from further down the alley. A dull thud followed.

"No, please!" A cry close to a sob preceded another thud.

I took a step closer to the end of the alley; it turned to the left out of sight. There was another shriek, this one full of pain. I ran toward the sound. Adrenaline pounded through my veins as I rounded the corner. I stopped short in shock.

Three men stood around a cowering boy; a fourth man leaned against the wall with a gleam of amusement in his eyes. He toyed with something dark in his hands and nodded at one of the others. The man lifted what looked like a table leg. The boy shrank away from him, his hands raised to protect his already bruised and bloody face. When he turned, my heart slowed. Brown and white feathered wings, battered and dirty, hung from his beaten shoulders. Clumps of feathers littered the alleyway.

My gut clenched. "Stop!" My feet moved before I knew what I was going to do.

All four men turned and the boy shrank back against the grimy bricks of the dead-end. "Mind your own business," the furthest man spat. He pushed off from the wall, his gaze narrowing. Anticipation coursed through my veins at the promise of an opponent. Instinct took over and I sized him up without breaking stride.

He stood at five-nine, an inch shorter than me; his frame was sparse and he walked with a swagger that told more of boast than fighting experience. The other three glanced from me back to him, awaiting orders. I wondered why they followed him because two of the three towered over six feet and the third looked like he could bench-press a bull; but still they waited for his word to take action.

"Leave him alone." My hands shook with rage as I closed the distance between us.

The men laughed.

"Why should we listen to you?" the leader asked, his voice as cruel as the gleam in his eyes. He glanced at his men; they started toward me.

11

Instinct screamed in the back of my mind, but I ignored it and raised my wings. Their eyes widened and the three men slowed; they looked back at their leader. I expected relief when I met the boy's eyes, but his expression now showed fear where only defiance and pain had been. He shook his head and tipped his chin, indicating that I should leave. Confused, I shook my head and looked back at the others. "You can't do this."

The leader turned so that he faced me directly; his three men backed to the walls on either side. "I've lost a fortune on you Galdoni." He lifted the object in his hand. I stared down the barrel of a gun and my blood ran cold. Before I could so much as flinch, he pulled the trigger twice. The first bullet skimmed the top of my left shoulder and passed through my wing feathers, but the second hit the bone just below my left wing joint.

A yell tore from my lips. I stumbled backwards with the force of the blow. My wing collapsed against my back; pain stole my breath and fogged my thoughts. I leaned against the wall for support.

The man gave a twisted grin and motioned with the firearm. "Not so tough now, eh?"

His men surrounded me. I pushed the pain to the back of my mind as I had been trained and stepped sideways to keep them all in sight. The beefy one hefted the table leg to his shoulder.

My muscles tensed. There would only be one chance. I threw a glance at the boy. "Run!"

"What?" he asked in surprise.

"Run, now!" I yelled. I turned and charged past the three men, diving at the leader with the gun. His eyes widened; he stumbled back and pulled the trigger as he fell against the wall. The bullet whizzed past my head and echoed down the alley as my fist connected with his jaw. I heard the boy run by and dodge the other men. I punched the leader twice in the stomach, then turned in time to duck the table leg aimed for my head.

I kicked one of the men. He gasped and doubled over. The man with the table leg swung it again. I let it pass inches from my chest, then put my weight behind a hard right to the man's jaw. He spun with the force of his momentum and my punch and fell to the ground.

I dodged a haymaker from the third man and turned back in time to see the leader groping for his gun. I couldn't see it in the darkening alley; I turned back just as one of the men threw a jab at my face. I ducked, punched him in the stomach, then threw my weight into a hook to his jaw. I moved to finish him with a quick chop to the back of the neck. A shot rang out; fire tore through my right leg just above the knee. It buckled under my weight and I stumbled with a gasp.

The beefy man hefted the table leg. I ducked, but was a hair too slow. The leg smashed into the side of my head and I spun and hit the ground. I pushed up slowly. Blood ran down my face. I shook my head to clear it from my eyes. A boot kicked me in the ribs at the same time that the table leg smashed into my back. I collapsed on the asphalt.

A foot stepped into view. I gathered what was left of my strength, then gritted my teeth and lunged. The man cried out as his knee buckled backwards. The satisfaction I felt was short lived when the table leg connected with my injured wing. I fought back a sob at the pain that clouded every thought. I dug my fingers into the pavement in an effort to keep from passing out.

Someone stepped on my back, flattening me to my stomach on the ground. A loud snap sounded and a knife-like pain flowed from my right wing to my chest; a yell tore from my throat. Another foot connected with my ribs and I felt them give.

"Not so tough now, eh Galdoni?" The table leg slammed into the back of my head.

Someone stood on my broken wing. Black feathers drifted past my cheek. Gravel bit into the side of my face and I barely felt another kick.

"Is he still alive?" the leader asked.

Fingers fumbled at my neck. "Barely," came the response.

The first man snorted. "Well, he won't be for long. Take 'em out of the Arena and they die just as fast as a human." His voice darkened. "Let's see if we can find the other one."

"Freakin' Galdoni messed up my leg," one of the men whined.

Their footsteps faded away. I couldn't clear my thoughts enough to take pleasure in the fact that the man had to be helped by his comrades in order to walk.

Ringing filled my ears along with a whooshing sound like how books described the ocean, only it was steady and growing. I knew that my life blood spilled around me, but I couldn't find the strength to care.

***

Pain intensified when I awoke. Each breath brought a sharp throb through my ribs. I gasped and doubled over in an attempt to make it stop, but the movement awakened deeper, searing pain in both of my wings. I opened my eyes but saw only a blur of darkness. I tried to sit up, then stifled a cry at the pain that jolted through my body.

"Hold still," a soft voice said. Surprise registered through the fog in my mind that the voice was female. A hand put a gentle pressure on my shoulder and eased me back down. "You're safe here."

"I can't see." I fought to keep my voice steady.

"The doctor said that might happen; your head was hit pretty hard."

Her words brought back the fight. It flashed through my mind as though I watched from a higher point of view. Shame filled me at the mistakes I had made, mistakes I knew better than to make. I should have done away with the gun in the first place and finished them without mercy. We hadn't been trained with firearms, but it was a stupid mistake; a deadly one. The crack of my broken wing and the sound of the shots echoed along with their laughter. Blood pooled around me and the memory went dark.

I reached up a hand to rub my forehead and found it wrapped in cloth.

"Are you thirsty?"

The answer was yes, more so than I had ever been in my life, but the taste of fear dominated the thirst. I looked toward the sound of her voice, but couldn't see anything past the black blur. "Where am I?"

"My friend Nikko's house. My brother Jayce, Nikko, and I found you in the alley. There was so much blood I thought you'd die, but Nikko's dad's a doctor. He came to help when we got you back here." I heard the scrape of a chair across a wooden floor. "Nikko told me to call him as soon as you woke up. Dr. Ray had to teach a class, but he'll be back."

I grabbed where I guessed her hand would be and found her fingers. She let out a small squeak of surprise but I didn't let go. I fought back nausea at the pain rolling in waves to the point that I almost blacked out again. "Wait," I managed to get out.

She held very still until the pain cleared enough that I could think again. I realized that my hold on her fingers was a lot harder than I intended and loosened my grip. "Sorry. It's just. . . ." I couldn't find the words to describe the way my heart pounded at the thought of strangers I couldn't see filling the room.

She seemed to guess my thoughts. "You can trust us. We brought you here because it's safe." I let go of her fingers and she stepped back. Her footsteps seemed to hesitate, then a door opened and they faded away.

The need to escape pulsed through my veins. I tried to sit up again and fought back tears as the weight of my bandaged wings pulled against the wounds. A splint kept my wounded knee straight. I eased it to the ground, then gritted my teeth and pushed up against the bed.

The second my weight settled on my knee, it collapsed under me and I fell to the floor. A cry broke from my lips as I hit the ground. I rolled to the side and fought to keep from losing control as wave after wave of pain and nausea coursed through my body. Hurried footsteps rushed down the hall. Muffled voices spoke quickly, but I couldn't make out the words past the roar in my ears. Darkness swarmed my mind and I gratefully gave in to it.

Chapter Two

Voices whispered in a low cadence nearby. Instinct kept me still as I slowly regained consciousness.

" . . . dangerous, what with the police declaring them suspects. You should turn him in."

"He's hurt, Dad, almost dead. You said yourself he shouldn't have made it through the night. Now you want to hand him over to them? They'd probably just let him die."

A few moments of silence, then, "You're putting everyone at risk."

"We know the danger. Everyone's had a say, but something doesn't feel right about all of this. Until they give us more information, he should stay. Please keep helping him."

A sigh. "Alright, but you need to be careful. Keep the door locked and don't let anyone in. He's still dangerous." The door opened and closed behind them and their voices faded away.

"They're gone," a soft voice whispered close by.

I jumped in surprised, then clenched my jaw against the pain.

A hand touched my shoulder. I fought not to shy away from it. "Sorry," she said, her tone genuine.

I opened my eyes and found to my relief that the darkness had lessened somewhat. I could make out a dim shape near the bed that moved with the sound of a chair creaking in protest. "How did you-" The words came out rusty.

Her voice showed her smile. "When you're awake, you breathe shallow because of your ribs."

I noted that for the future. "You're quiet."

"I've made an art of it." Her tone softened but she didn't expound. She turned away and my throat burned at the sound of water being poured. "You must be thirsty. Dr. Ray said you could drink as much as you wanted when you woke up."

A straw touched my lips and I sucked gratefully at the water until I heard a gurgle of air.

"Wow, thirsty," she said. "I'll get you some more."

I shook my head, then put a hand to it to stop the spinning. "No, I'm okay." I pushed up from the bed, slower this time.

"What are you doing?" she asked in alarm.

I held my ribs and leaned forward into a sitting position. "I've gotta get outta here."

"You can't!" She took a step back. "You'll be killed if you're found; I'll go get Nikko."

I shook my head quickly, then leaned my forehead against the side wall to stop the nausea that followed. My wings ached with every movement, but I kept myself from wondering whether I would be able to fly again. I definitely wasn't in a good enough mental state to consider what I would do otherwise. "Wait, please. I can't stay. You heard that guy. I'm a danger. You shouldn't have brought me here."

I felt the bed lower when she sat on the corner. "You would've died."

I fought back the impulse to say I wasn't afraid of death. The phrase had been drilled into us at the Academy, and I thought I believed it until death had actually stared me in the face. Anger rose in my chest. "They would have killed him if I hadn't stopped them."

"Who?"

"A boy; they were beating him because he was a Galdoni." My lips curled in disgust. "They had a gun, and he was afraid to fly away." I stared in the girl's direction, angry beyond the attack itself. That simple act had shattered my every hope of the world outside the Academy.

We sat in silence for a minute, then the girl gave a low chuckle. It was a pleasant sound that chased away my dark thoughts. "What?"

"You wouldn't get very far, blind with two broken wings and a shot leg. Where'd you plan to go?"

I gave a small, wry smile at the thought. "I don't know. Not far, huh?"

"Definitely not far."

I turned one of the pillows so that I could lean against the wall and face her without putting pressure on my wings. They ached with the movement, but I ignored the pain.

"Why'd you help me?"

"We couldn't just leave you there." Her tone was one of amazement that I would even suggest it. Then her voice brightened. "Hey, I don't even know your name."

I thought about it for a minute. "Kale," I answered cautiously. "What's yours?"

"Brielle, but everyone calls me Brie." She sat in silence for a minute, then said, "You know, you're different than I thought."

Her curious tone caught my attention. I knew I shouldn't encourage her to talk to me; my presence put her in danger, but talking to her kept the pain at a bearable distance. "Different, how?"

The bed moved as she shifted her weight. Her movement made a sharp stab of pain race from my knee up my thigh, but I didn't show it. "Well, Galdoni are supposed to be savage, brutal fighters. Animals, really; at least, that's what they tell us."

A knot began to form in my stomach. "Who's they?"

"The Arena reporters. They say it before and after every show." Her voice darkened. "I think it's to make sure people don't think of Galdoni as human, because you're killing each other." She paused, and then said in a quieter tone as though uncertain she should continue, "According to the reporters, Galdoni were a failed genetic experiment. You only want to kill, which is why you were chosen for the show."

Bile rose in my throat. I swallowed hard. "We were made, not chosen. We're trained to fight, to not be afraid. But I didn't know it was for some show." I didn't hide the disgust in my voice. My head started to throb.

"Not just *some* show, the most watched television show in the world. People throw away their life savings betting on you guys."

"Betting on which one of us will die?" The implication made my stomach roll. It had never occurred to me to question what we did at the Academy. None of us did. Training and fighting was all we knew; but what Brie said brought it all into a perspective I wasn't prepared to face.

I saw the Academy for the first time from a profitable point of view. There was too much to consider at once, but jarring details swirled through my mind like the forbidden questions, the separation of ages, the restrictions. I gripped the blanket beside me until my knuckles ached.

Her voice quieted. "There're a lot of groups out there making waves, saying that it's unethical. I think that's one of the reasons it got shut down; that and a rumor about some of the big wigs skimming money off the top to pad their own pockets."

I nodded silently. When they had shut down the Academy, all we had been told was that we were to be given a chance to make our own way in life; but if what Brie said was true, they must have lost millions, if not billions, just by letting us walk out the gates. Exhaustion clouded my thoughts. I closed my eyes.

"You should sleep," Brie said quietly. I felt her weight rise from the mattress. "Do you need help lying down?"

I wanted to tell her no, but I was already too far into the void to respond. I rested my head back against the wall and gave in to the fog that swarmed through my thoughts.

***

The next time I awoke, my limbs burned with fever. Chills wracked my body even though blankets had been piled on top of me. I could barely make out the voices that spoke around me, strangers in the dim room. I couldn't hear Brie's voice among them; I wondered if she had finally realized how dangerous I was and left.

***

I had no idea how many days had passed when I finally opened my eyes and found the fever gone and my blurred vision somewhat lessened. The room was blissfully empty and my throat burned with thirst. I pushed up slowly to a sitting position. The movement made my wounds ache, but it also verified that I was alive. I could take pain.

The blurred shadow of a pitcher stood on the dresser a few feet away. I moved my bad knee to the edge of the bed and rose carefully, keeping my weight on the good leg. My wings throbbed with the movement, but whoever had bandaged them had wrapped them securely to my back to keep them immobile. I leaned on the bedpost, then limped along the wall to the dresser.

My body shook with fatigue by the time I reached it. I couldn't do more than laugh weakly when I picked up the pitcher and found it empty. I turned to go back to the bed; low voices caught my attention. I limped the few steps to the door and opened it carefully so the hinges didn't creak. The conversation grew louder.

"They're arresting anyone who hides them. We'll be thrown in jail as accomplices," a male voice said in an urgent tone.

"Accomplices to what?" Brie answered, her voice defiant.

"Do you really want to know?" he demanded.

"Okay, Jayce, calm down. It's not like we have to decide anything now," another male replied calmly.

"And wait for the police to come pounding on your door? Everyone's at risk here; you know that, Nikko!"

"Did he look dangerous to you?" Brie asked. "We're lucky he made it through the last few nights, and he acted surprised when I told him about the show."

"You told him?" Jayce let out a chortle. "That's rich. Way to clue him in on his role here!"

I gritted my teeth, but kept my mouth shut.

"That's enough, Jayce," Nikko's voice cut in. "He's not dangerous right now, and we can restrain him if we need to. There's just too much going on for us to make a hasty decision. Dad said he won't even be strong enough to leave the bed for another few weeks if he survives the fever. We'll make a decision then if things become too intense."

The sound of someone sitting down not so gracefully was followed by Jayce's slightly calmer voice. "Fine. And until then, I'm sleeping with my knife under my pillow."

I smiled, but Nikko's next words wiped the smile from my face.

He spoke quietly. "Did you see the scars he has? What do you think that means?"

"Probably that he kills people. I don't believe his story about the boy in the alley," Jayce commented darkly.

"We saw the brown and white feathers," Brie told him in an exasperated tone as if they had gone over the same thing before. "We have no reason not to believe him."

"Yeah, except there was an awful lot of blood in that alley, and I don't think it was all from him."

I frowned and tried to remember if I had hurt any of them enough to draw blood. I hoped so, but doubted it.

"That doesn't mean anything," Nikko pointed out.

"It means you have a dangerous Galdoni in your house whose presence puts everyone in danger. That's not something we should fool around with."

He was right. I knew the danger better than they did. I pushed open the door and a hinge creaked. The trio looked at me; I could make out the blur of them sitting on two couches. Brie rose to her feet.

24

"Kale, we-"

"I need to leave. You're right. I'm a danger and it would be best if I left your home." I leaned against the door frame to catch my breath.

"You don't need to leave," Nikko said. He rose to stand beside Brie. "Jayce is just being himself." He glanced at his friend.

Jayce's voice lowered. "I didn't mean for you to hear that. We're just worried, that's all."

"And with good reason. They've got to be out looking for us by now, what with the millions they've apparently just thrown down the drain. I shouldn't be here. You should have left me in that alley." I closed my eyes and rubbed the bandage across my forehead in an effort to stop the headache that was starting to pound.

"Brie," Nikko said cautiously, but she didn't listen.

Brie crossed the room and ducked under my arm so I could lean on her. My ribs gave a sharp ache at the movement. "You need to sit before you fall down," she said, pulling me to walk with her.

I fought back a protest and limped to keep most of my weight off her. She eased me down on the couch next to Jayce. I kept my leg out, but the pressure of my wings against the back of the couch made me wince and I had to sit forward. The world spun. I took a deep breath to fight down the nausea and leaned my head in my hand. When my stomach was under control again, I glanced at Jayce. He had turned to face me, a cushion between us. I gave him a wry look. "I'm not going to kill you or anything, if that's what you think."

"Reassuring," he replied, staring at me. "I'll bet that's what most killers say before they slay their victims."

"Jayce!" Brie and Nikko said in unison.

I shook my head. "It's okay. 'We fear things in proportion to our ignorance of them'."

"That's a Livy quote!" Nikko stared at me.

I nodded. "Politics at its barest."

He exchanged a glance with Brie. I took a shallow breath. It made me uneasy how quickly my strength failed. I wouldn't get far in such shape. I flexed my knuckles and noticed for the first time that they were scraped and bruised.

"That must have been quite the fight," Nikko commented.

I glanced at him and nodded.

"Did you kill anyone?" Jayce asked. Brie slapped his shoulder but he ignored her, his attention on me.

I went with the truth. "I didn't kill any of them."

He then asked the question I dreaded. "Have you killed anyone?"

I didn't answer. It was something we never talked about at the Academy, kill records and death. It was all supposed to be just practice, but accidents happened and punishment for such accidents never took place. The closer we got to the Arena, the fiercer the battles became.

I felt Jayce's stare and pulled my thoughts back to the present. My mind worked sluggishly through an exhausted haze. "It's kill or be killed at the Academy, but I never wanted to hurt anyone." He fell silent for a moment and I glanced at him. "You don't believe me." I said it as a statement, not a question, but I was surprised when he shook his head.

"I do believe you." His tone showed his own surprise. "I've always been able to tell when someone's lying, and you're not lying." I felt the cushion dip between us as he leaned closer. "What's it like at the Academy? I've heard rumors, but no one ever goes in or out. How long has it been since they've let anyone leave?"

26

"Twenty-nine years," Nikko and I replied at the same time. I glanced at him, but couldn't make out his expression with my still blurry eyesight. I shrugged and ignored the pain it brought from my wings to my shoulders. "We were raised in the Academy; this is our first time seeing the outside."

"Raised? I thought you guys came out as adults, blood thirsty and fighting," Jayce said, a hint of embarrassment in his voice.

I glanced in his direction. "Not exactly. We're what you'd call test-tube babies." I looked down at my bruised knuckles. "Combat is a religion at the Academy. We live it, breathe it, and know that some day we'll die from it if we're not fast enough or strong enough to defend ourselves."

"But you know Livy," Nikko said quietly.

I nodded. My heart clenched at the memory. "Academy professors smuggled books to the few of us who held interest in the world outside. They also held secret classes at night. I think they were hoping we could change things eventually, if we had enough insight into our own situation and the outside world."

"What's your favorite book?" Brie asked. Her tone was carefully neutral and I wished I could see the expression on her face.

"*The Count of Monte Cristo* by Dumas," I told her.

Nikko laughed. "That's ironic."

A smile spread inadvertently across my face. I was about to reply when a footstep caught my attention. I rose quickly despite the aching protest of my wounds.

"What is it?" Brie asked, alarmed.

"Someone's coming." I backed toward the door, gritting my teeth when I forgot about my knee and put weight on it.

The front door opened.

"Dr. Ray," Jayce said.

"Hello students, how-" I felt his shock when he saw me. "What is going on here?" he roared. He stalked toward me and I limped back until I felt the door behind me. Adrenaline surged through my veins and my body tensed for attack, but I fought it down. "You get back to that room and you stay there! You put these kids' lives in danger just by being here. If anything happens to them, so help me, I'll-"

"Dad," Nikko protested. He grabbed the doctor's arm. "He's okay, really."

"He might have you fooled," Dr. Ray growled, "But he's a trained killer and a suspect in a government conspiracy. I should have known better than to agree to him staying here."

My head swam. I stepped through the doorway and limped backward toward the bed; instinct screamed for me not to turn my back on him.

"But Doc, he hasn't done anything," Jayce argued, surprising me.

The doctor's voice lowered. "You should keep your sister out of danger. You know better."

I sat on the bed and pushed back so that I could lean against the wall. My head throbbed and my knee ached. I could feel the damp bandages where it had started to bleed again. The exhaustion that weighed down my limbs made my thoughts sluggish. I struggled to stay upright.

The doctor came into the room and shut the door behind him. He took a step toward the bed.

"Don't touch me," I growled.

He paused, a dark blur in the dim room. He spoke in a professional, reserved tone. "I need to look at your knee; it's bleeding again and you might have done some more damage to it walking around."

I shook my head. "I'll take care of myself. Thank you for your assistance, but I no longer require your care."

The doctor stood still for a minute. I thought he would leave, then he sighed and took a step closer. I raised my hands, ready to defend myself, but he shook his head and grabbed the back of the chair Brie had used. The legs screeched against the floor as he pulled it back to sit near the wall. He settled onto it and crossed one leg over his knee.

We sat in silence. I glared his way despite my blinding headache.

He finally sighed. "I think we got off on the wrong foot."

I refused to comment.

He put his leg back down and spread his hands. "You have to understand my point of view. These kids are my responsibility. If they were harmed in any way, I could never forgive myself." He dropped his hands to his knees. "Regardless of if you are personally a danger to them, your presence here puts us all on the line."

The honesty of his words ate at my distrust. I nodded. "I need to leave."

He snorted. "Not like that. Despite the way I might feel, I'm still a doctor." He gave a low chuckle. "I'd be a great example throwing you out on the streets in your condition."

"You'd be preserving your safety," I pointed out.

He shook his head. "I wouldn't be a doctor if I didn't have empathy. You need to stay." He sighed and leaned forward. "Tell you what, I'll take care of your wounds and you teach us about the Academy. I have the feeling there's a lot that went on there we don't know."

I felt his gaze on the scars that stood out across my bare chest. I crossed my arms, self-conscious for the first time in my life.

"What do you think?" he asked after a minute of silence.

I didn't have much of a choice and I think he knew it. I finally nodded against my better judgment. "I'll stay, but the second the danger to anyone here increases, I'm gone."

"I can respect that," he said. He rose and held out his hand. I hesitated, then took it. His grip was firm. "Now, let's see to that knee."

Chapter Three

I slept through the next day and awoke to the smell of
food and the sound of laughter from the next room. I sat up
slowly. The ache in my ribs had lessened somewhat. I moved
my knee so I could lean with a pillow against the wall. The
new splint Dr. Ray had put on helped lessen the pain, but it
throbbed whenever I used my leg muscles. I pushed the
constant ache of my wings to the back of my mind.

I longed for a book, though my eyesight was still blurred
to the point that reading was impossible. I smoothed the
pillow, and noted how soft the pillowcase was. Nothing was
soft at the Academy. I bent gingerly toward the small table
beside the bed and picked up the clean pair of clothes Brie
had set there for me. The fabric was also soft and supple,
quite different from the coarse pants at the Academy.

Footsteps came to the door and I tensed.

"Kale?" The door opened to reveal Nikko's brown hair
and slender build. He came in when he saw I was awake.
"You hungry?"

My stomach growled at the strong scent of food that
wafted in after him and he laughed. "Good enough. Why
don't you come out and eat with us? Brie and Jayce's dad had
to work late again, so they're here."

The thought was surprisingly inviting, but I shook my
head. "Dr. Ray-"

"He's not here," Nikko replied firmly. "Dad teaches
during the day, and when he's not teaching, he's at the
emergency room. The odds of him catching us are slim."

Before I could protest, he swung my arm over his
shoulder and helped me to my feet. "You've gotta be ready to
get out of this room anyhow, and we've run out of Galdoni
rumors to chew up. It'd be nice to have a little fact to even

out the fiction." He helped me slip the shirt over my head. Brie had cut two slits up the back that fit around my wings; the fabric settled comfortably against my skin.

We made our way out the door and into the small living room. The couches had been pushed aside and a card table and folding chairs made up the dining table. Brie pulled out a chair so I could take a seat. Nikko helped me ease down onto the chair, then left to the kitchen.

"You should be starving," Brie pointed out. She handed me a roll before following Nikko.

I held the bread in my hands. I wanted to tear into it, to shove it into my mouth and devour it completely. But in the house setting, that felt wrong. It took more self-control than I wanted to admit to take a small bite.

The fresh taste of bread filled my mouth with more flavor than I thought possible. I closed my eyes and savored the sweet tang of cooked flour and sugar. I rolled the bread around my mouth for a moment before swallowing it. The lightest hint of honey lingered on my tongue.

I opened my eyes and took another bite just as the Nikko and Brie entered the room with bowls of mashed potatoes and gravy and a salad along with a pitcher of juice. Jayce followed closely behind carrying a roast in a pan. My stomach growled again at the smell and Nikko laughed.

"Hurry and feed this boy before he starves to death!" He proceeded to plunk a generous helping of potatoes drowned in gravy onto my plate. The others served me and then themselves, ignoring my protests that I had plenty of food. I finally gave in and sat back to watch them dish food onto their own plates in far less amounts than mine. After dishing up, they looked at each other.

A slight discomfort seemed to pass between them. "What?" I asked.

Nikko cleared his throat. "We generally bless the food before we eat."

I nodded.

Jayce glanced at me before he bowed his head and said a prayer.

I watched the three lowered heads and fought back a strange wave of longing. It felt surreal, sitting at a normal table with a home-cooked meal in a comfortable home. It was something I had read about in books and longed for when I was younger; I had accepted my lot long ago only to find myself in the same situation.

"Amen," Jayce said. He looked across the table at me and though I couldn't see his expression, I heard the caution in his voice. "I didn't take you guys for the praying type."

I shrugged and pretended to be more interested in my potatoes. "We don't as a whole, but I've read about it. I always found the idea of God to be an interesting one."

"Not one you believe in?" Brie asked.

I glanced at her and shook my head. "It was never hidden from us that we were created by humans, definitely not God; though it fits the description of playing God." I'd had more time than I wanted in the last three days to think over what Brie had told me about the televised Arena broadcasts. The knowledge took the honor that we as Galdoni had been taught our entire lives and thrown it down the drain. I fought to keep the anger from my voice. "I'm a little skeptical at the thought of an all-knowing Being who sees what we go through in our lives but lets injustice carry on anyway."

Silence followed my words.

Jayce chuckled, breaking the stillness. "Why don't you tell us how you really feel?"

I rubbed the bandage on my forehead. "Sorry. I'm not usually this blunt. My head must have been hit harder than I thought."

This time Nikko was the one to laugh. "Hey, at least you're honest. Most people don't have a clue what they believe or don't believe. It's kind-of refreshing."

"In a knife through your heart sort of way," Jayce concluded. He held up his cup of juice. "Here's to brutal honesty."

I laughed and held up my own. When the glasses chinked together, I realized it had been years since I had truly laughed; I had also smiled more in the last few days than the rest of my life combined. A voice in the back of my mind told me not to get used to it. I tried to shrug it off, but the pain that laced through my wings when I moved reminded me of what had brought me there. I took another swallow of juice to chase down the bitterness that rose in my throat.

***

"How does that feel?"

"Better," I replied and tried not to wince as the doctor tightened the bandages around my wings. He bound them to my back, immobilizing the joints to allow the bones to heal.

"You have a high tolerance for pain," he noted.

"One of the benefits of the Academy," I replied quietly.

Dr. Ray gave me a careful look as he tore the end of the bandage and smoothed it down. "Well, I can't guarantee anything, but it should hold for now." A rare hint of humor touched his voice, "Must say, I never thought I'd be bandaging up a Galdoni."

"That makes two of us," I said with a wry smile. At his pause, I clarified, "I never thought I'd have to be bandaged by a human."

A chuckle escaped his lips as he turned away to tuck the rest of his equipment into his bag. The shadows were lighter and colors sharper; faces were still mostly a blur though. I rubbed my eyes. My head ached, but less than it had when I first awoke.

He must have been watching me. "Your eyesight should come back. You've already made good progress." He paused, then continued as though testing the water, "You haven't asked about your wings."

I looked at him, but didn't reply.

He finally shrugged. "Well, it's probably for the best. I won't know until those bandages come off, and until then, it's a guessing game for both of us." His tone became ironic. "You know, there's one reason I became a doctor instead of a vet."

"Why's that?"

"Because it's easier when the patients can tell you what's wrong with them. But," and I could hear the smile in his voice, "You never say."

"Habit, I guess."

Brie opened the door and we both turned. "Hello gentlemen; don't mind me. I just brought the invalid some water."

I snorted at the term invalid, but accepted the cup she held out.

"I'll see you tomorrow." Dr. Ray picked up his bag and made his way to the door. "Have a good night, Brie." He paused before turning back with a slight frown in his voice. "You too, Kale."

The doctor left before I could get over my surprise enough to wish him the same.

Brie laughed and sat on the corner of the bed. "I think you're breaking him down. You're definitely not the 'maddened beast of mass destruction' they tout on TV to get you guys back to the Academy."

"You don't think so? I'm pretty terrifying."

"Yeah, to a mouse maybe, or a gerbil. I'd say a guinea pig, but I hear those things can fight for themselves."

I chuckled. The movement shot pain through my ribs; I leaned back against the wall. "How was school?"

"Splendidly boring, as usual." She let out a sigh. "You're lucky you don't have to go."

"I'll trade you, Academy for high school."

"Done. I can learn to fight and have wings, and you can sit in a hard chair learning about things you'll never use in life."

"At least the goal is for you to have a life when you're done. Imagine finding out that they taught you everything just

36

to have you use it to die for the enjoyment and monetary interest of impassive viewers."

She let out a breath. "Okay, you win."

I smiled. "Hey, if it wasn't for you, I'd probably still be there, or dead."

"Probably dead," she replied flippantly; I could see the slight outline of her grin. "Now you have to put up with all my whining about school. You'd probably rather I left you there."

I tipped my head as though considering it and she slapped my good knee. I smiled. "No, I'm really more grateful for you than I could ever express. I just can't wait until I get out of here. Something has to be done."

"Like what?"

I shrugged because that was as far as I always got. Something had to be done, but where to start? I scratched at the bandages on my forehead. The deep gash Dr. Ray had stitched there itched. "Something; I don't know what, but I'll figure it out."

"You'll know what to do." Doubt colored her voice.

"You don't think I should go back." The revelation surprised me.

"To what?" She sat up straight and her tone became passionate. "You have a chance to start a new life. I think you should take it and never look back."

"And leave the other Galdoni to whatever fate the Academy has for them?" I shook my head. "I can't let them continue to spread lies about us and let people believe that we don't feel or care. I need to stop them from killing the Galdoni I grew up with."

They weren't friends. Galdoni were forbidden to have friends. If such a relationship was discovered, the two offenders were beaten and then separated for the rest of their time at the Academy. But I had grown up beside them, trained against them, and at the barest of it all, survived with them. I couldn't let them suffer for things that should have been stopped long ago, and the fact that Galdoni were being returned to the Academy by every defense unit available meant there was a plan to put them to use again.

"You're right," Brie replied quietly.

My wings ached and I longed to stretch them. I shifted against the pillow, but couldn't find a comfortable position. I finally gave up.

Brie guessed my thoughts. "You want to fly?"

"More than words can describe." I glanced at her. "You know, I've never flown outside the Arena. None of us had until they shut it down, and then I was scared."

We stared at each other, both surprised at my admission. I grimaced. "Now I'll be lucky if I even can. Last time I look before I leap."

"I'll bet you'll be able to fly," Brie said reassuringly. "And if not, there's more out there."

"Like what?" I asked skeptically.

She was close enough that I could see her mischievous grin. "Nikko thinks you should go to school with us."

"High school?" The thought made me laugh. "They'd arrest me on sight."

"He thinks we can hide your wings, and Nikko is a whiz at computers. He can make you a transfer transcript that'll get you in."

I stared at her in disbelief. "You've got to be kidding. It wouldn't work, and it'd be dangerous for everyone if I'm caught."

"Well, it's just a thought," she said casually.

I shook my head. "I won't be here that long. There's too much to do."

She nodded. "And research to be done. You can't rush into this, Kale. You've got to know your enemy."

I didn't answer. It was too absurd to even consider. Nevertheless, sleep was a long time coming after she left.

Chapter Four

When I made my way to the table the next night with the use of a crutch Nikko found, I was surprised to see Dr. Ray waiting patiently on an extra chair pulled up to one of the corners. He nodded at me and resumed his conversation with Jayce.

Brie's brother glanced at me with a slight shrug and a concerned expression. He brushed away the blond hair that was always in his eyes and turned back to the doctor. I took the seat next to him as nonchalantly as possible. Brie and Nikko followed from the kitchen a few minutes later. They both looked stressed at the doctor's presence.

Brie said a brief prayer and I caught the doctor's glance after she finished. "Nikko mentioned your views on religion," he said, dishing a generous heap of stuffing onto his plate.

I glanced at Nikko but he kept his eyes down.

"The only religion taught at the Academy is the art of combat," I replied carefully.

Dr. Ray nodded. "Interesting. You know, the ancient Samurai's battle training was closely entwined in their religious views."

"So I've read."

The doctor motioned with his fork for me to continue. I toyed with the corn on my plate. "From the moment of creation, Galdoni are put through rigorous training regimes which are eventually honed toward each Galdoni's skill. We were required to fight a personal and group battle at least once a day, unless we were recovering."

"Recovering?" Brie cut in, "From what?"

I glanced at her. "After we master weapons training, all combat is fought with real swords, knives, or whatever the battling Galdoni chose."

"Real weapons?" Jayce leaned closer, "You mean sharpened and everything?"

I nodded and held out my left arm. A jagged scar ran from the base of my elbow to my wrist. "It took me almost a month to recover from this one, but they had me fighting again the next week."

"That's barbaric," Brie exclaimed with a shake of her head.

"It's survival," I replied. It surprised me how impersonally I could talk about the Academy. It had been my entire life. Now, it seemed more like a nightmare I could remember instead of one I had lived every day.

Even Dr. Ray looked appalled, though I know he had seen the scars all over my body. I flexed my hands, glad to see that the bruises on my knuckles had faded along with my blurred eyesight. I looked up and met the doctor's gaze across the table.

His expression was thoughtful but troubled. "Nikko's mentioned that he found a way to get you into the high school if you're interested."

My stomach clenched, but I kept my face carefully expressionless. "Really."

Nikko, Brie, and Jayce looked from one of us to the other.

"I think it might be a good idea."

Shock flowed through me at the doctor's approval. "You do? I . . . I don't know if it's very smart."

"Why not?" Nikko piped in. "This is your chance to live a real life. You can leave all the Academy stuff behind and decide what you really want to do."

I shook my head. "I already told Brie why I have to go back. There's no choice in the matter."

Jayce raised a forkful of food and pointed it at me. "You always have a choice. Besides, it's not like you can go back like that. If you're planning for a fight, you'll have to get into shape again. That could take a while and you might as well put your free time to good use."

I looked at the doctor. "You said yourself that the Galdoni are dangerous and shouldn't be trusted. You want one around your students?"

He chuckled. "You've already been around my students." His expression turned serious and he put an arm on the table. "I judged too quickly in ignorance. You're a kid like the rest of them and deserve the same opportunities. If anything, you have more self-control than anyone else your age."

"Hey," Jayce protested. He knocked a cup over with his elbow and sent orange soda across the table. Brie rushed to mop it up with paper napkins.

"Thanks for proving my point." The doctor's brow creased. "Imagine all you could learn."

I didn't answer because I knew there was too much they weren't considering. They changed the topic and continued with the meal, laughing and chatting about the day and leaving me to my own thoughts. I finished my food in silence, thanked the doctor for his hospitality, and left to my room with more questions than I had the night before.

***

Jayce lounged on the couch, his fingers entwined behind his head. "So you're like a black belt; your hands are considered deadly weapons, right?"

I shrugged from my place on the other couch. I couldn't sit back because of my wings, but it was better than my bed. Sleep had eluded me the last few nights thanks to worrying about the preparations Nikko was making. Against my better judgment, I had finally given in to their arguments about school. Nikko was having a heyday with the planning. I felt butterflies in my stomach for the first time in my life.

"I guess so. We studied so many types of combat I don't know what you'd call it."

"I'm just glad you're on our side." Jayce picked up the open can of soda he had set beside the couch and raised it to me before he drank.

"Me, too," I agreed. I toyed with the tassels on one of the couch pillows.

Jayce chuckled. "Nervous about your first day of high school?"

As much as I didn't want to admit it, I nodded.

He grinned. "Don't be. It's not like they're out to get you. You'll have the advantage."

I raised an eyebrow. "Oh, and what's that?"

"You get frustrated, you can just fly away." He glanced at the bandages on my wings and shrugged. "Well, soon anyway, hopefully."

"Hopefully," I echoed. I couldn't allow myself to consider what would happen if not.

"Well, don't worry. Tomorrow we'll get everything straightened out and you can start your first day of school

Wednesday." He sat up and gave me a critical look. "We need to get you cleaned up first."

I hadn't been able to take a decent shower since the attack. Thankfully, Dr. Ray had created coverings for my damaged wings so I could have a real shower in the morning. Obviously I wasn't the only one looking forward to it.

"Brie can cut your hair." At my incredulous look, he grinned. "Don't worry, she cuts mine, Nikko's, Dr. Ray's, and our dad's. She's actually pretty good." He gave me another, closer look and nodded. "You're close to Jayce's height and build, beside the wings of course. I'll take charge of the clothes."

I sighed. "Do we really have to do this?"

He rose from the couch and slapped my good knee in passing. "Don't worry, man. I really think you'll like it. It'll be an adventure." He left through the front door and I watched him walk across the street to his house.

"I've had enough of those for one lifetime," I replied under my breath. I pushed to my feet and crutched my way back to the bedroom. Between the crutches and the wings, Jayce had better come up with a pretty convincing outfit.

***

I eased down into the small bathtub, careful to keep the bandages at my wing joints dry. The hot water eased the aches that had never quite gone away. It was the first bath I had ever had, and though I had been skeptical at first, I now understood why Brie said a hot bath could be the ultimate stress relief. But I was still glad I didn't stoop far enough to let her put bubbles in the water. Jayce would never have let me live it down.

I felt like a part of the filth that came from my past at the Academy washed away as I cleaned my skin with the hot water and minty soap Brie had provided. I studied the scars that stood out in stark contrast against my skin. I again felt the lashes and weapons that had carved their signatures into my body.

Somehow, being away from the Academy, acting somewhat human, felt like leaving the last bite of pain from those wounds in the bath water. I didn't dwell on the fact that I wasn't human and could never be. It was enough just to be part of something civilized, to feel like I was at least somewhat in control of my own life.

I scrubbed my body until I finally felt clean. My black wings gleamed, the feathers finally clear of the dirt and grime from the alley so that they glinted dark purple at certain angles in the light. The bandaged joints ached whenever I moved, but I hoped it was a healing pain. I combed the tangles out of my black hair. It hung to my shoulders, longer than I usually wore it, and drove me crazy by constantly falling in my eyes. Maybe a haircut would be a good idea.

I pulled on the jeans and black collared shirt Jayce had set out. It took some doing to ease the new slits in the back of the shirt over my wings, but when I had it settled, the clean

GALDONI

cotton felt good against my skin. Dr. Ray had removed the stitches from the gash on my forehead earlier that day; I traced the healing line above my eyebrow.

My gaze shifted so that I stared at the stranger in the mirror. He looked back with dark eyes, a firm jaw, and something unfamiliar on his face. Hope. I shook my head and turned away. I would need more than hope to get through tomorrow. I opened the door and used a crutch to make my way into the living room.

Brie sat by herself on the arm of the couch, a comb and scissors on her knee and an empty chair in the middle of the floor. Her eyes widened when she saw me. My stomach turned over strangely at the look on her face.

"You clean up nice," she said in a tone I didn't recognize.

"Thanks."

I stopped by the chair and set the crutch on the ground. Brie sat quietly for so long I finally looked over at her. When she met my eyes, a touch of red colored her cheeks. I frowned slightly, uncertain, and she stood up, dropping the scissors and comb to the floor.

"Go ahead and take a seat," she said. Her face was hidden by her long brown hair as she stooped to pick up her tools.

I sat and tried to ignore the fact that I was about to let a near-stranger close to me with a potentially dangerous weapon. Her footsteps crossed behind me and stopped for a minute. I jumped at the feeling of fingers lightly brushing one of my wings.

"Sorry," Brie said, her voice quiet. "You're wings are beautiful. I've never seen feathers like these."

She ran the comb through my hair. The feeling made me want to stay in the chair forever and fly away and never come back all at the same time. My muscles tensed and I had to force myself to hold still.

46

"Relax," Brie said gently. She combed the hair back from my forehead, her fingers soft on my skin. "I'm not going to cut you, I promise."

I nodded and she said with a slightly teasing note in her voice, "Well, I might cut you if you move your head. Hold still, but don't be so tense. Trust me."

It took a surprising amount of willpower to close my eyes. I took a deep breath and let it out slowly. The soft snip of scissors was followed by the almost inaudible sound of hair falling to the floor. Brie ran the comb through my hair again, followed by another snip. She started to hum softly to herself, so soft that I doubted she even knew she did it. The music calmed my frazzled nerves and took the tension from my shoulders.

"That's better," she said quietly.

I opened my eyes to see her staring inches from my face. Her gaze followed the strands of hair she measured with her fingers. She met my eyes for a second, then continued on, a slight smile on her lips. I memorized her smile.

"Did anyone tell you that you have amazing eyes?" she asked as she moved around to the back.

I was about to shake my head, then remembered her warning. I gave a rueful smile. "Not exactly a high topic of conversation in combative society."

I heard the answering smile in her voice. "Well, you do. They match the color of your wings in certain light."

Her fingers ran from my forehead to the back of my hair, measuring lengths. I closed my eyes again and concentrated on the soft touch. So little in my life had been gentle that I had to fight from tensing against the surprise blow my body assumed would come. I had never realized how many walls I had up until Brie's touch threatened to crack them all.

I became aware that the humming and cutting had stopped; I opened my eyes to find Brie sitting on the couch across from the chair, her brow furrowed and brown eyes serious. "When was the last time someone cut your hair?" she asked quietly.

I rolled my shoulders despite the pain it brought and leaned forward to put my elbow on my good knee. I studied the faded outline of bruises on my hand. "Never. I do it myself." I glanced up only to see her frown deepen.

"Does anyone take care of you guys over there?"

"At the Academy?" I asked, though it was obvious. She nodded and I shook my head. "We take care of ourselves. Dependency is a sign of weakness, or so they tell us." I pushed myself to my feet. She picked up the crutch and held it out. My hand brushed hers when I took it and I paused as a jolt of electricity ran up my arm at her touch. I took a calming breath and settled the crutch under my arm, then gave her a half smile. "What would they say if they saw me now?"

"Do you really care?"

Her question caught me by surprise. I glanced at her. "You are forward, aren't you?"

She brushed her hair back from her face with an impatient gesture. "You shouldn't care. Really. Look at what they did to you. They meant to send you out there to die. You don't have to go back. You don't have anything to prove. It'll be a death sentence."

Her words echoed the argument that had swirled in my head the past few days. Anger at my own lack of answers surged through me. I gritted my teeth before I said anything I would regret.

But she saw it. "What? Tell me."

I shook my head and turned to go back to my room.

48

Brie caught my arm, her grip firm. "Kale, I helped save your life. You owe me that much."

The way she said my name made me turn back against my will. She must have seen something in my face because she let go of my arm and stepped back. I took a breath and tried to push away the pent-up fury in my chest. I leaned against the arm of the sofa.

"It's what I'm meant for, Brie." I ran a hand through my hair. It felt good to have it shorter. I shoved the hand in my pocket. "It's all I know. I've been taught to fight my whole life, and now, here I sit and wait to heal for what end? How can I do anything the way I am? Who are we kidding thinking I'll fit in at this school? And what happens to you guys when we're caught? It would have been better if you'd let me die out there."

Brie's eyes widened; I looked away. She took a step forward. "You don't really believe that, do you?"

She tried to hide the hurt she felt, but I could hear it in her voice and hated myself for it. I lowered my head. "I believe it for you, for all of you. You shouldn't have gotten caught up in this."

"We chose to, and we accepted the risk. We aren't kids, Kale. We know what we're doing." At my glance, a faint blush stole across her cheeks again. "Well, at least most of us know what we're doing." She sat down on the couch and motioned for me to join her. Her gaze was soft and trusting. Knowing what she did of my background, I wondered why she dared to be in the same room with me, let alone ask me to stay. I frowned but took a seat against my better judgment.

She sighed and toyed with a small beaded bracelet around her wrist that I hadn't noticed before. "Can I tell you something?"

I gave a small, guarded nod. "Yes."

49

She looked at me carefully. "Promise you won't tell Jayce?"

"You have my word."

"Our parents, well, my step-father." She hesitated, but I nodded encouragingly. She looked down at her hands. "He has a drinking problem and he gets violent. I want to get my sister away from them."

"How old is she?" I had never tried alcohol; it was a banned substance at the Academy for obvious reasons, but I had read about its uses and effects.

"Eight. When my parents divorced, my father won custody of Jayce and me, but Allie was so young that they let her stay with my mom. I almost didn't go with Dad because I was so worried about leaving her, but Jayce talked me into it. He said if we could establish that this was a better place for her, we would eventually be able to take Allie away from it all." She glanced at me and I could see the worry in her eyes. "But when I spoke to Mom on the phone yesterday, she mentioned that Rob lost his job."

"And you're worried his drinking will get out of control," I finished her thought. She nodded, her eyes bright with concern. I knew I should reassure her, but her reasoning made sense. "Does your sister know how to reach you if things get out of hand?"

"She has my cell number, but it's a two hour drive. Dad's gone for the next few days on a business trip and I worry about something happening while he's gone." She rubbed her eyes tiredly. "Maybe I worry too much. Jayce thinks everything's okay." Her voice dropped softer. "But he never really felt there was a problem in the first place. Even when Rob was beating on Jayce, he figured it was better than Rob beating Mom or me."

"But now there's no one else to beat on," I replied.

She nodded. "It keeps me up at night. Jayce thinks I worry myself sick for nothing, but I can't help it. I can't wait to get her out of there."

"I can't blame you. You're a good sister to worry."

She gave me a grateful smile. "It's nice to have someone else to talk to about it. Thanks for understanding."

But I didn't, really. I had never been concerned for another person besides myself. At the Academy, it was fight or die. There wasn't room for chivalry or mercy.

"What's it like, having a family?" I asked, curious.

She gave a slight frown. "Mine isn't the best example, really. My dad's away on business all the time. We've practically lived here at Dr. Ray's since the divorce, but it's better than living at my mom's. Jayce, Nikko, and I have pretty much become our own family." She glanced at me. "But it's nice to have someone you know is there when you need them."

"I'll bet," I replied quietly.

She gave me a kind smile. "I know you don't have the whole family problems thing, but you're a good listener." She rose and offered me her hand. "You need more sleep, and I could use some myself. Tomorrow'll be a big day."

I took her hand and made it to my feet. Though I didn't need the help, she led the way to the bedroom and opened the door. I crutched past her and eased down on the bed.

"Be careful," she said with a teasing twinkle in her eyes. "You might get comfortable here."

"We wouldn't want that," I replied, only half-joking. I reached for the shirt and shorts Nikko had given me to sleep in.

She grinned and started to close the door behind her, then paused. "Kale?"

"Yeah?"

51

"I'm glad you're here." She shut the door behind her and left me in a darkness that didn't seem quite as thick as usual.

Chapter Five

The scent of books, old carpet, strange food, and a smell similar to workout socks met me when we stepped into the school. I stared at the flow of students rushing around us and jostling each other as they made their way to their classrooms. Two students bumped into me, then stumbled away laughing and holding onto one another. Brie touched my arm and smiled. I took a steeling breath and followed them into the chaotic throng, reminding myself that we were safe as long as no one figured out what I was.

The anxious glances Jayce, Nikko, and Brie exchanged as we made our way down the hall toward our first class weren't lost on me. To my surprise, the black trench coat Jayce gave me to hide my wings didn't raise any eyebrows. He said it was an older style, light enough to blend in with the rainy weather, and short enough that it didn't bring to mind a mass murderer, which he stated with a humorous twinkle in his eyes. I was tall enough that with my wings bandaged tightly against my back, there was only a slight bulge against the loose cloth. I hoped the casual observer would take it as just an odd fit of the coat.

Jayce kept glancing around as if worried about something. I put it off as concern about sneaking me into school, but the look on his face and the way his eyes darted down each hall we passed put me on edge. He caught my look and leaned over, "I kissed a girl last week and now her brother's out for my blood."

The words sent a thrum of anticipation through my veins. We were almost to the classroom when a tall student with short red hair spotted us through the crowd. My muscles tensed at the look on his face, but he ignored me, his eyes on

Jayce. Two students, obvious acting as his backup, followed him toward us. "Jayce, I'm gonna-"

I stepped in front of Jayce, grabbed the student by the shoulder and shirt, then threw him headfirst against the lockers. He crumpled to the ground in a motionless heap. Jayce stared from me to the unconscious student, then grinned at the student's two wide-eyed companions. They turned and ran back up the hall.

"That's right!" Jayce yelled after them. "You'd better run if you don't want to end up like Dane!" He slapped me on the shoulder, awe bright in his eyes. "Thanks man, that was awesome!"

Brie's brow was creased and she opened her mouth to say something, but a shrill bell rang above us.

"Come on," Nikko said in an exasperated tone. He threw another glance at Dane. The student had pushed up to his hands and knees and stared at the thin carpet as if wondering how he had gotten there. The locker above him was dented. Nikko shook his head and entered the classroom with Brie close behind.

Dr. Ray nodded at me on our early entrance to his class. We took seats on the furthest row and I watched the other students file in.

"That was awesome," Jayce said breathlessly from the seat in front of me. "He didn't even touch you! I need you around more often!" He held out a hand palm up.

I stared at it, uncertain what he wanted me to do.

"Give him a high-five," Nikko said dryly from the chair behind me. "Not like he deserves it or anything."

Jayce glowered at him. "You know she kissed me first. Dane overreacted, like usual; at least I don't have to worry about him anymore."

"Unless he seeks revenge, or Kale gets expelled. A great move for a first day," Nikko argued.

Jayce rolled his eyes. "You know Dane's not going to blab to the principal. He's already lined up for a suspension if he's in another fight." He held out his hand again. "You high-five like this." He slapped his palm with his other one, then held it up again for me to do the same. I slapped his hand and he grinned.

Brie shook her head from the seat next to me. "Boys," she said before turning back to her book.

Dr. Ray watched us with lifted eyebrows. I dropped my gaze and ran a hand along the cold table, tracing the names carved into the top.

It felt surreal to meet the semi-interested gazes of the other students, only to be dismissed as just another newcomer. My heart hammered at the secret I hid. Jayce threw me a glance when the bell rang and everyone was settled; I realized he felt the same way.

Human anatomy rushed by in a blur of facts spoken in Dr. Ray's calm tones. We waited for the rest of the class to file out at the bell; I rose feeling like I had conquered something.

"See, piece of cake," Nikko said.

"I could use some cake right now," Jayce replied.

I didn't know how he could think about food; my stomach was in knots with nervousness.

"Just breathe," Brie said at the look on my face. "It's going to be alright."

Dr. Ray nodded at us when we walked past his desk. "Have a great day, guys," he said with a humored look.

Students rushed past us to their next classes while Brie showed me where my locker was and Jayce unceremoniously dumped the book Dr. Ray had given me inside. Nikko kept looking around; I knew he was concerned about Dane.

"I'm not worried about him," I said quietly on our way to the next class.

"I know," Nikko said, throwing another glance over his shoulder. "But Dane doesn't mess around. Once he has you in his sights, he never lets up."

I shrugged. "I can take care of myself."

He gave me a frank look. "You're not the one I'm worried about."

I fought back a smile at his tone, but Brie grabbed the sleeve of my jacket and pulled me to the side of the hall so the students heading to class could flow around us. "We'll catch up," she said to Jayce and Nikko. They walked far enough down the hall to not overhear, then waited near a drinking fountain. Brie sighed and turned back to me. "Look, you can't do that here."

"Do what?" I asked, surprised.

"You can't fight, and you can't hurt students the way you did Dane."

"He'll be okay," I replied, my brow furrowed at the intensity of her tone. "I was protecting Jayce."

"Jayce deserves what he gets," she said. My eyebrows rose and she sighed. "Fighting isn't how we resolve things around here. It's not civilized."

Her words sent a stab through my heart. I wondered how words could hurt so much; I fought to hide the emotion. "Then how should it be resolved when Dane's obvious intention was to hurt Jayce?"

She glared up the hall at Jayce. "By talking it out or not doing the deed in the first place. Jayce knew better than to kiss Janice, but he loses his mind around pretty girls."

"So he needs to work it out himself?" I hazarded.

She gave a slight frown. "It'd be a good lesson for him, but I'm afraid Dane won't give up. You'll have to watch your back."

"I'm used to that," I replied.

She nodded and I followed her to Jayce and Nikko. Jayce and Brie left down the next hallway to math, and I followed Nikko to the biology class we shared.

Long white tables scattered with microscopes filled the room. Posters of dissected cartoon animals, a diagram of photosynthesis, and slides demonstrating mitosis lined the walls. A whiteboard covered in rough sketches of plants stood behind a long wooden desk.

The teacher, a slightly balding, tall, skinny man with glasses and a sincere smile motioned at us from across the room.

"Mrs. Bean said we had a new student." He glanced around the room and pushed his glasses up the bridge of his nose with a finger. "We don't have any free microscopes, so you'll have to work with Nikko. He can fill you in on what we've done so far."

He motioned for us to take our seats, then picked up a sheaf of stapled papers from the corner of his desk and raised his voice so the class could hear, "Today we're studying the fourth stage of mitosis which is anaphase. The chromosomes will be moving to opposites sides of the cell so that it can prepare to split. Look in your microscopes, identify any cells in anaphase, and draw them on your paper. You should have the first three phases already identified."

I glanced at Nikko; he grinned and whispered, "Don't worry; it's easier than it sounds." The teacher dropped a stack of papers on our table. Nikko picked them up, took the top two pages, then passed the rest down to a girl with long red hair pulled into two braids.

I studied the paper for a minute before scooting the microscope closer. The images were blurred, but Nikko showed me how to adjust the focus. Little circles suddenly appeared. A smile pulled at the corners of my mouth as I looked for the cells in anaphase.

***

I met Brie outside of the English class we shared. She gave me a smile. "How'd it go?"

I hefted the biology book. "I've got a ton of catching up to do, but Nikko says he'll tutor me. I did like the microscopes."

She made a face. "Just wait until they make you dissect a frog." She went into the classroom and I followed her to the back row. An older lady with short, gray-streaked black hair set copies of books on the desks. She wore a red shirt and gray skirt with a black sash around her waist.

The teacher gave me a kind smile as she handed me one of the books. "Welcome. You're fortunate to join us in time for *Macbeth*." She leaned closer and said in a loud whisper, "Just don't think you can watch Mel Gibson and get the gist of it. Several of your peers tried that with *To Kill a Mockingbird* and didn't fare very well."

"Hey," the boy in front of me said indignantly.

The teacher shrugged. "I warned you, Ryan. I've watched the movies, too."

The student next to him elbowed him when the teacher walked away; they both started laughing.

I ran my fingers through the worn pages of the book, amazed at how easily they were handed out. Ryan grabbed his copy and shoved it into his backpack without noticing how the pages bent. I cringed, thinking of how difficult it was to get books at the Academy. We had been forced to hide them with great care. If any were found, it meant beatings and confinement for the student, and the teacher was never seen again. I lifted the pages to my nose and inhaled the dusty, worn scent of faded ink on old paper. Brie glanced at me.

Embarrassed, I set the book back on my desk, but she smiled and smelled her book, too.

"The last student who read this either had a smoking habit or lived with smokers," she said, setting it quickly down. I laughed and the teacher threw us a warning glance. We fell silent as she began to read the first chapter of the book aloud.

"Does she say it out loud because some of the other students don't know how to read?" I asked after class. We met up with Jayce and Nikko at the end of the hall and walked together to the next class we shared.

Brie laughed. "They can read, but so many failed the test on *To Kill a Mockingbird* that she's convinced reading it in class is the only way anyone'll get through it." She glanced at Jayce. "And she might have a point."

"I read it," he exclaimed. At her look, he shrugged. "Well, the first page, a couple in the middle, and then the end. But," he said with a triumphant grin. "It was enough to get me a C minus!"

Brie shook her head. "How on earth do you expect to pass your sophomore year settling for a C minus?"

"That's all you need," Jayce replied. "Besides, I'm acing history and economics, so it'll even out."

Brie and Nikko exchanged an exasperated look as Nikko held open the door to our history class. The teacher, a short, bald man with glasses, was busy writing facts on the whiteboard in various colors of markers. I was surprised to see that he wrote everything without referring to a textbook or notes.

There were designated desks, so Brie and Jayce sat near the front while I took an empty seat by Nikko at the back. I heard a humming sound and realized it was coming from the teacher as he finished the last of the notes and swiftly dotted a few i's that he had missed. He then turned with a flourish and waved at the board.

"Copy this down. It will be on the test next Friday. Also, read Chapter Seventeen and it wouldn't hurt to brush up on some weapons of World War I while you're at it." He wiped his hands on the front of his vest, then sat down at the big wooden desk and pulled out a paperback book that didn't look at all history related.

I glanced at Nikko. He gave me a thumbs-up and proceeded to copy down the notes. I fought back a wry smile and did the same.

***

By the time the bell rang and we broke for lunch, I felt like I had truly accomplished something. I was surprised at what the students were learning. I would be hard pressed to catch up, but it was a good feeling, like I had an interesting challenge to complete that wouldn't result in mastering a new way to kill someone.

I followed the others through the lunch line and was amazed at how much noise a lunchroom full of students could make. We carried trays loaded with foods I had never seen before to a circle of grass outside. I leaned back against one of the trees and breathed in the fresh, rain-washed air that chased around us. I propped my injured leg on my crutch and poked at the food on the tray.

"So how'd your first official day of school start?" Jayce asked, biting into a pile of gray and brown gravy-covered noodles.

"Very interesting. I feel like an undercover spy learning national secrets or something. It's weird."

Brie grinned at me over her salad. "Don't worry; you'll get bored of it soon enough, especially with Mr. Derby's art class."

They all groaned and Jayce kicked Nikko's foot. "What'd you put him in that for?"

"Dad thought art would be a good outlet, and Kale said he was interested in broadening his horizons."

"Mr. Derby'll broaden them, that's for sure," Jayce replied with a wince.

I shrugged. "Bring it on. The more I can learn while I'm here, the better." I finished my tray of questionably smelling French fries, apples covered in cinnamon syrup, and peas which actually tasted quite wonderful. We dumped our waste in the garbage can near the doors and handed the trays to a lady with a hairnet and an expression on her face that said she would hit someone over the head with the said tray if they forgot to throw their plastic ware into the recycle bin.

We turned down a side hall and Nikko held open the door to economics. We settled on the back row, a theme I noticed they followed in any classroom without assigned seating. I was starting to feel confident that we had actually pulled it off when I caught a look Nikko threw Jayce.

"What?" Jayce whispered.

Nikko sighed and gestured to the whiteboard.

'The Galdoni Impact on Our Economy' was written across the top in red marker. Bullet points and a graph showing the jump in tax money collected since gambling was legalized for the show fifteen years ago were drawn in blue and green. I glanced at Brie and saw her reading the bullet points, her lips a tight crease.

"Alright students," began the teacher, a woman with tightly-curled, short blond hair and blue eyes hidden behind cat-eye glasses. She smoothed the front of her calf-length brown dress. "We have a new student in class. Some of you may have met him already, but please say hello to Kale Matthews."

She motioned to me and a few boys said disinterested hellos while several girls turned to look at me; I felt for a moment like a bug under inspection. Three girls gave shy smiles with little waves while a pair in the front corner turned back and started giggling.

The teacher ignored them and jumped into her lecture. "As we began to discuss yesterday, the Galdoni impact has been more markedly felt in the past month and a half since the program was discontinued. Because of this and the government's steps to take care of those individuals that misused the funds set aside for the program, the Arena is being reopened. There are some who feel that closing the Arena for this short stint of time was planned. Does anyone have an answer as to why that might be?"

A boy with short black hair and stars buzzed into the sides of his head raised his hand. "Supply and demand," he said.

"That's right," she continued. "As the supply runs out, the demand increases. I expect that when the Arena airs again, twice as many people will be inclined to gamble on the outcomes."

A girl with chin-length brunette hair raised her hand. "Isn't it illegal for the government to hold a monopoly on the program?"

The teacher shook her head and began a discussion on needs versus wants and their places in the economy. I zoned out her high voice, lost in the mind-numbing thought that the Arena was reopening. Reason dictated that it was only a matter of time, but the time had come quicker than I imagined. I didn't hear the bell ring and Nikko had to nudge me when the class was over.

***

The intermediate algebra class I shared with Brie went quickly. Math had always come easily to me; it was taught at the Academy to calculate variables, increase attack efficiency, and for better energy management and preservation during a fight. I was actually able to show Brie a few shortcuts on the problems and it felt good to at least know something in one of my classes.

Jayce and Brie held back smiles when they left Nikko and I at Mr. Derby's Art class. I took a seat at one of the long white tables next to Nikko and promptly found out why.

"A new student!" the teacher said. He was a skinny man with wild brown hair and red glasses. He adjusted a white apron covered in paint splatters, then held out a hand. "Mr. Derby, at your service."

"Uh, Kale," I said, glancing at Nikko. He just grinned and sat back to watch.

"Kale, you are welcome to our class!" He waved an arm to indicate the entire classroom which was very slowly filling with students who only seemed to perk up when they noticed the teacher with a new student. "Here we learn how art and color coincide to create magic." I lifted an eyebrow and he laughed. "Exactly, my boy!" He turned to the rest of the class and clapped his hands. "Places, places. Let the magic begin!"

Nikko pulled out a rough charcoal sketch he was working on of an old barn next to a magnificent oak tree.

"You did that?" I asked, amazed.

He nodded, sliding a plain sheet of paper toward me. "Make whatever you want. Mr. Derby isn't specific. He just says to make it magical." He rolled his eyes with a barely suppressed smile as Mr. Derby came back to our table.

"Exactly, Mr. Ray! Exactly. Make it magical. I couldn't have put it better myself." He beamed at Nikko and glanced at his picture. "Ah, I simply love that tree. Love it! It will look beautiful on our wall!" He waved his hand with a flourish.

I turned to see a wall filled from top to bottom with pictures from students. Not a single inch of the wall showed through, and the pictures were several layers deep as though instead of removing one to put up another, they were just placed on top. He glanced at me over his glasses. "I'm hoping Mr. Matthews will have something to add as well."

I studied the blank white paper; it matched the current state of my mind given the task at hand. "I'll try," I said uncertainly. I had never made anything creative in my life. The Academy frowned on individualism, and any sign of wavering from the strict studies was swiftly punished. I picked up the charcoal with the feeling of breaking some unspoken rule.

"Don't try, do," Mr. Derby said. His enthusiasm was catching and several students around us grinned. "Do your best and your best is what you will do." He left with a nod as though satisfied by his words.

I glanced at Nikko. "Do my best?"

He grinned. "And your best is what you will do."

I laughed and twirled the charcoal between my fingers. The blank paper stared up at me as though daring me to smudge its perfect whiteness.

I was still staring at it a few minutes later when Mr. Derby wandered back. "Haven't found your muse?" he asked.

I shook my head.

He gave a thoughtful frown and pulled at his lower lip. "Whenever I have trouble thinking of what to make, I look through my past for an image that stands out above the rest, something that defines me even though I may not know why."

I glanced at him in surprise and he smiled. "Even art teachers have a serious side." He winked and walked away.

I found Nikko staring at me with a confused look. "I didn't know he had a serious side," he whispered.

I stifled a smile and stared down at the paper. The white purity faded and I saw the Academy gates as I left them, the silhouetted forms of Galdoni flying over the top, picketers ringing the fence, and the hulking gray form of the Academy building standing empty and menacing behind them.

It would be a dead give-away, but perhaps I could draw something similar. I took a deep breath and began to sketch an outline of wings. The charcoal glided over the paper leaving long, stark lines; a faint whisper of satisfaction rose in my chest.

***

Dr. Ray met us at home that night. "A successful first day, I gather?" he asked with a glance at all the books I had spread out on the card table.

I nodded and turned back to my work. He took the chair opposite me and studied the books thoughtfully. "You know, I didn't think you'd actually go through with it. The type of social situation you're in at the Academy doesn't exactly lead to experience in a normal classroom setting."

"In other words, you thought I'd chicken out?" I surmised.

He nodded with a twinkle in his eyes. "Your nonchalance in my classroom was either really good acting or a very quick adaptation to unusual situations, both of which are rare for someone your age."

I grinned at him. "Just good acting. I thought my heart would beat out of my chest. And I had to keep reminding myself that I couldn't fly away if things went terribly wrong." I rubbed my forehead and tried to put my feelings into words. "I found myself actually missing the mapped out days at the Academy; a tight schedule with high security and barely a breath of free time. The freedom feels almost too good to be true. It makes me feel scattered, if that makes any sense."

He gave an answering smile. "One day successful. Most of human life is spent living one day at a time. We don't have every hour mapped out for us. It's what we do in our unscheduled time that makes us who we are."

"It feels unstable, like there's too much choice and opportunity to mess up." I glanced at the books. "But I think I finally understand what Benjamin Franklin meant when he said, 'Those who can give up essential liberty to obtain a little temporary safety-'"

"'Deserve neither liberty nor safety,'" Dr. Ray finished with an approving smile. "Yes, liberty is bought at a high price, but in the end you'll see it's highly rewarding as long as you learn to spend your time wisely."

"Something that's never been my own 'til now," I mused. "It'll take some getting used to."

Brie walked in the front door with Jayce close behind. "What will?"

"Time," the doctor and I said together.

Jayce gave a dramatic sigh. "Don't tell me Dr. Ray is catching you on *and* off the clock with his professional rants."

The doctor gave him a patient smile. "The things you could learn if you but had the patience to sit and listen, Jayce."

"I do way too much sitting and listening in school as it is to hear more of it when I'm home. Do you want to wear Kale out on his first day?"

"Jayce," Brie chided.

Dr. Ray rose from his seat and patted her shoulder. "No worries. For a student interested in law, Jayce has a fairly flippant attitude toward the educational system. We'll just hope it doesn't rub off on his feelings toward true justice."

Jayce grinned and ran a hand through his blond hair. "It already has. Why else do you think I plan to minor in drama? I'm going to need some help acting interested in some of those ridiculous cases. Justice? More like waa-fest," he concluded with a dramatic sigh. He fell on the couch and glanced over at me. "Speaking of justice, Kale's been rubbing elbows with Dane Daniels.

Dr. Ray's eyebrows rose. "Rubbing elbows?" He turned to me. "You mean fighting?"

Jayce laughed. "I don't think I'd call it fighting. More like Dane throwing punches and Kale redirecting him to the floor."

Dr. Ray frowned. "School bullies are something I didn't plan on." He glanced at me. "You managed to keep from killing him?" His tone was only half-joking.

I nodded. "Dane obviously hasn't had any training, and I just let his momentum carry him into a locker. It was kind-of refreshing knowing I could beat him and not doing it, if that makes any sense."

Nikko walked into the room. "If what makes any sense?"

"Kale was just telling me about Dane," Dr. Ray explained.

Nikko nodded with a concerned frown. "I hope Dane can be smart enough to back down when he knows he's over-matched."

The doctor shook his head. "Lucky for us, Kale has self-control to counter his lethal training, but I need the rest of you to act as a buffer between him and the rest of the school. Dane shouldn't have been able to get near him in the first place."

"Sorry, Dad," Nikko apologized. He looked at me with a hint of awe in his eyes. "But Dane came looking for a fight and Kale's instincts were to protect Jayce; he shut him down before any of us could move."

It was weird to watch Nikko and Jayce defend me even though I was in the wrong and knew it. My instinct was to take down an attacker regardless of his target; Jayce just got lucky, but I couldn't bring myself to tell them that.

Dr. Ray frowned. "You never know what course of action a bully will take, especially when his pride's at stake. Promise me you'll keep Kale out of his way from now on."

Brie and Nikko nodded with apologetic expressions; Jayce sighed as though he had enjoyed seeing Dane meet his match, but at the doctor's look, he quickly agreed.

Dr. Ray turned back to me. "Let's check your wings. It's time to change the dressings and I want to test your range of motion." He walked to my room and left me to follow.

Brie gave me an encouraging smile. I took a deep breath and crutched after the doctor. He closed the door and motioned for me to sit on the bed. I lifted my splinted knee and turned so that my back faced the doctor.

"I think we've both been putting this off," he said as he carefully worked the bandages from my feathers.

I nodded, my throat tight. I hadn't let myself think about what I would do if I couldn't fly. No matter what the Academy did to us, I wouldn't give up my wings for a normal life. I didn't know if it was the bird DNA in my blood, but the call of the wind haunted my dreams.

I gritted my teeth as I felt the doctor loosen the last of the bandages and lift the padding free from my left wing, the one that had been shot. I forced myself not to ask questions and hid a wince at his gentle prodding. He lifted the wing joint and carefully extended it a few inches. I bit my lip at the pain and tried to ignore the hope that rose when the motion was even possible.

"Mmmhmm," Dr. Ray said before he applied a salve and covered it with a new set of bandages. He then turned and checked the right wing which had been broken just above the shoulder joint. "It's been five weeks now, too soon to know exactly how it's healing. But the splint's held and the bones were set straight before it was bound." He patted my shoulder. "Keep them immobile for a few more weeks and I have reason to believe you just might fly again after all."

I pushed down the hope that rose in my chest at his words and forbade it from showing on my face when he finished binding the wings close to my back. I turned around slowly.

He must have seen something in my eyes, though, because he gave a small smile. "You know, it's okay to hope just a little, Kale."

I shook my head. "It's better to face reality. Right now, I can't fly. I don't want to let myself believe I might again just to have it taken away." I clenched and unclenched my jaw against the rise of emotion in my chest.

Dr. Ray nodded. "As you wish. But our ability to hope is one of the things that set us apart from the animals. Looking toward a brighter future can give us the strength we need to get through our trials."

I gave him a small, ironic smile. "Well, fortunately for you, you're a lot further removed from those animals than I am." I motioned toward my wings. "The animal inside me warns against looking toward the intangible. That way, if it becomes unattainable, I won't have thrown my life away for something I could never have in the first place."

Dr. Ray tipped an imaginary hat. "Touché. Maybe between the two of us, we'll find a happy medium in this unpredictable world."

"I hope so," I heartily agreed.

He grinned at me and left. I worked my tee-shirt back on. The others had set the table by the time I made my way back to the living room. My mouth watered at the smell of dinner.

"Who would have thought a day of sitting in classrooms would make me so hungry?" I mused out loud.

Jayce snorted. "Now you know why I'm always eating."

"Yeah," Brie replied with a smirk. "But you eat the same amount during the breaks."

"Breaks make me hungry, too," Jayce said. As if to make his point, he scooped a generous helping of spaghetti onto his plate, and then doubled it. "Perfect."

"Perfectly disgusting." Nikko sat across from Jayce and helped himself to some garlic bread.

"Where's Dr. Ray?" I asked.

"He had a class to teach," Nikko said with a shrug.

"And our dad's working late again," Jayce said around a mouthful of spaghetti. "So it's another night of 'kids, fend for yourselves.' We get that a lot."

"Because there's not enough food in the world to keep you fed," Brie said.

Jayce threw a piece of bread at her and she laughed.

I found myself watching them, the way they bantered as if they knew each other so well no one would take offense. Words like that would spur a usually life-threatening fight at the Academy. I found it hard to wrap my mind around their easy acceptance of each other's faults and idiosyncrasies.

"Kale?"

"Yes?" I asked, jolted back to the present.

Jayce smirked and Brie smiled. "I just asked if school met your expectations."

"Exceeded," I replied. I motioned with my fork, a habit I'd unconsciously picked up from Jayce. "It's amazing how much you're taught every day. It must take some practice to remember everything in time for a whole new day to start tomorrow."

"You think we remember everything?" Jayce said with a laugh. "It generally goes in one ear and out the other, then we have to cram it back in for the tests."

The others laughed and nodded in agreement. "The goal is to graduate," Nikko said. Jayce looked at him in surprise, and I wondered if they had argued the point before. "After we have our diplomas, we can start our own lives. This is a holding point until then."

My brow furrowed. "But this is your lives. If you keep waiting for the 'after', you'll miss everything that happens now."

Brie nudged me with her elbow. "That's what I keep telling them. I think they'll catch on eventually."

Chapter Six

The weeks flew by. Galdoni were being arrested and brought back to the Academy. We caught every scrap of news about the Galdoni round-up we could find. Rumors continued about the Arena reopening. They released statements that the Galdoni were a danger to the public and that they needed to be used for the purpose for which they were created. Galdoni were considered a national threat, and anyone found hiding them were prosecuted as accomplices.

Reporters claimed that funds from the Arena were going to be reallocated toward the building of new city centers. Nothing surfaced about the Academy's lawsuit and the original closing. Even Nikko's research came up empty. The only real facts he found hinted that the charges were being dropped toward some of the major officials, and that the fights were to start up again soon. It seemed like the drop in gambling and cost of relinquishing the Galdoni hurt more than initially projected.

I expanded my studies with Dr. Ray to better understand what they did to create us. The splint on my knee was eventually removed, and though I still limped, the doctor promised that the pain would go away with time.

"Now about those wings. I took the splints off yesterday. Have you taken the chance to try them out?" Dr. Ray studied me intently.

I hesitated, aware that Brie and Jayce watched from the other couch. A pit formed in my stomach and I shook my head.

"Nervous?" Dr. Ray guessed.

At my lack of answer, he gave a knowing smile. "Many of my patients are afraid to test their limbs after their casts are removed. It's normal. But in your case, it's the only way to see if what we did worked. I know you have to do this in your own time, but try to have some faith."

I smiled at him. "One of your other intangibles."

"Well then, if you won't give me hope, belief, faith, or prayer, you'll truly have to do it on your own. Good luck with that." He nodded at the others and left the room with a chuckle.

Brie pushed away from the table. "I'm tired of studying. Does anyone want to get some fresh air?"

My head hurt from all the cramming, and I breathed a silent sigh of relief that someone else felt the same way. "Definitely."

Nikko laughed. "Two weeks of school and you're already acting like a student." He pointed his pencil at me. "But beware; once you start slacking, it's all downhill." He put the pencil behind his ear and sat back with a biochemistry book on one knee.

Brie shook her head. "Jayce's slacked off for years and he still hasn't reached the bottom of the hill."

"I heard that!" Jayce shouted from the kitchen. The refrigerator door closed and a can of soda cracked open. I fought back a grin.

Brie grabbed my hand and headed for the door.

"Hey, Kale."

I turned back in time to catch the coat Nikko threw at me. I stared at it for a second, horrified that I had almost left the house without covering my wings. At my look, Nikko smiled. "Don't worry about it. We all start losing our minds after hours of studying. You need to get out. Fresh air'll do you good."

I shrugged into the light trench coat and followed Brie out the door, my heartbeat a bit louder than usual.

I had felt myself slipping over the past week. My dreams were filled with images of flying. Even now, the wind toyed with my hair as if beckoning me to follow it. My wings ached, but I was afraid to use them, afraid to find out that they hadn't healed correctly; I was afraid to be neither human nor Galdoni. I had barely slept because of the dreams, but they had started to haunt my waking hours as well.

Unaware of my torment, Brie slipped her arm through mine and we walked in the twilight toward the forested area near the school. A light fog twisted slowly between the trees like lace sliding through a woman's fingers. Brie talked about her day and I let the words settle over me in a soothing balm.

We stopped at the bridge that crossed a deep chasm through the woods. I could hear water far below, but the fog stood almost level with the lips of earth on either side of us and obscured the bottom.

"It looks like you could jump off and float forever," Brie said, her voice dreamy.

I stared at her.

"What?" she asked. When I didn't answer, she smiled at me. "You've been quiet. What are you thinking about?"

"Desperate thoughts," I replied quietly.

She watched me for a moment as though to gauge whether I was kidding, then her eyes widened when she noticed the trench coat I had discarded on the railing. I couldn't remember how it had gotten there, but the rush of the breeze through the feathers of my wings felt more like hope than I had ever let myself experience.

"Kale?" she asked.

Before she could stop me, I was standing on the railing staring down into the bottomless fog. It swirled below like whipped cream melting in a cup of hot chocolate.

"Kale?" her voice rose, alarmed.

"I can't live like this, Brie," I whispered, my eyes on the ravine.

Before she could protest, I jumped.

The damp wind rushed past; moisture clung to my clothes and filled my senses with its heady aroma. It took all my effort not to close my eyes and let it end there, my last thoughts of the wind and welcoming darkness.

"Kale!" Brie's scream reached me and I opened my wings.

Pain laced through them at the unexpected force. I closed them for fear that they would break again. The sound of the river below roared in my ears. I fought past the fear and opened them enough to catch the wind that rushed by me. At first, it felt as though the wings were useless. The bottom of the ravine sped closer with them open, and a grim chuckle sounded in my mind at the irony. Then the wind caught and they lifted, filling with air as though they had never been damaged. I skimmed just above the river; it splashed on my face and I laughed once in triumph.

It felt so good to fly. I glided above the water, challenging myself with the dark twists and turns through the fog that tried to tear me from the air. I kicked off a large rock and shot upward. My wings ached, but it felt good, so good, to beat the air down and rise above the ground, above the trees, above the clouds to the stars. I soared for a few minutes high in the dark sky.

A peace I had never known before filled my heart. I breathed the crisp night air and held it in until my lungs burned. I let it out with a laugh and flew in lazy circles.

The bell tower near the school tolled below, breaking through my reverie. I remembered.

"Brie."

I dove heedless of the dark night and foggy trees until I saw her silhouette on the bridge. She stood on the railing, her hands clutching the support wires and her eyes on the fog below. My heart slowed at the gleam of tears on her cheeks. I landed quietly on the road a few feet away.

No one cried for me. No one had ever cried for me; nothing I had done ever instilled that type of emotion in anyone. I hadn't been made to cry for.

I took a step forward, fighting the pressure in my chest. "Brie?" I asked quietly.

She turned, and the relief on her face felt like the sun after a long rain. "Kale!"

She jumped down from the railing and ran the last few feet between us. She threw her arms around me and held me tight. I stumbled back on my bad knee, but managed to keep standing. Her tears soaked through my shirt and my soul. "Oh, Kale. Don't ever, ever do that again. Promise me."

"Brie, I-"

She looked up and glared, the expression comedic with the tear trails down her cheeks and the way her mussed hair circled her face, but I couldn't smile. I only saw the hurt in her eyes, the sorrow that she thought I would leave her like that after everything, the loss as one who only dares to hold on to so little feels.

I stepped back, my heart barely beating. "Brie, you can't look at me like that. You can't . . . you can't feel about me like that." I struggled to keep my emotions in check, to fight past the feeling of a fist encircling my heart.

"And you can't go diving off bridges with a death wish," she said, her hands knotted into fists and her eyes burning into mine. "You can't believe that flying is the only thing there is. You just can't."

"It's all I've got," I replied; my voice catching.

"No, it's not. You've got me; you've got all of us." She wiped a fresh tear off her cheek. "You've got me," she repeated.

"I-," I didn't know what to say. I rubbed my forehead, then threw my hands down in frustration. "I'm not worth all that."

Her eyes softened and she grabbed one of my hands. "Kale, look at me."

I shook my head, afraid of what my face would show.

She put a hand on my chest, her fingers gentle. I looked back, surprised, and she stood on her tiptoes so that her lips touched mine.

Fire ran from her lips and filled me with such intensity my breath caught in my throat. I kissed her back, carefully, slowly. My hand lifted of its own accord and tangled gently in her hair. Her lips smiled in response and she lowered her head so that it rested under my chin.

It was all I could do to stand there. My knees threatened to give out, and not just the bad one. The scent of her perfumed hair filled my senses and drowned out my thoughts. I put my arms around her, afraid to let go and afraid of hurting her at the same time.

"Your heart's racing," she said in a whisper after a few minutes had passed.

"It's going to explode from my chest," I replied when I was semi-confident my voice would remain steady.

I could hear a smile in her voice. "Is it from flying or from me?"

"You, mostly," I replied. I felt bare, stripped, as though honesty was the only thing I had left to offer her.

She tipped her head up and looked at me. "Does that mean flying's not as grand as you remembered?" Her tone was teasing.

I shook my head. "Even better, but nothing like you."

She smiled and stepped back without letting go of my hand. "Good answer."

A thought came to my mind. It was the only thing I could offer her, the one piece of my soul that hadn't been smashed to bits at the Academy. "Fly with me."

"What?"

"Fly with me. Let me show you." At her hesitancy, I smiled, my heart lighter than it had ever been. "Do you trust me?"

"Of course," she answered without hesitation.

"Then let me give you the only thing I have to give."

She walked beside me back to the railing and stood where I had jumped off a few short minutes before, minutes that felt like an eternity of my life had past. I put my arms around her waist.

"Ready?"

"Are you sure you're strong enough?"

I beat my wings up and down and felt a grin spread across my face at the power in them. She nodded and we jumped.

I pulled up shorter this time, surprised that Brie didn't scream or fight against the fall. She merely clutched my arms around her waist and waited. I heard her breath catch as the wind filled my wings and carried us up and over the fog. I pushed down hard and took us above the cloud cover to the star-filled sky above.

"Oh, Kale," she whispered.

I smiled at her, her eyes on the sparse view of the buildings through the clouds. Her brown hair tangled in the wind and when she glanced back at me, her eyes were alight with the stars and the shine of the moon on the clouds.

I pushed my wings harder and farther than I probably should have, but it was worth it to finally fly free, to soar without walls or chains or fear, to just give in to the flight.

When we finally landed behind Nikko's house, Brie stood on her tiptoes again and brushed my lips softly with hers. She smiled as though she couldn't smile big enough. "That was wonderful," she breathed.

"Then it won't be your last time," I replied. I didn't know why I said it, or why my heart gave an unexpected thump at the way her face lit up, but I knew at that moment that what was left of my heart was no longer my own.

She took my hand in hers and walked slowly toward the front of the house.

The second we crossed into view of the windows, the front door opened and Jayce burst out, his eyes sparking with anger. "What do you think you're doing?" he demanded. He threw something on the lawn and charged down the stairs.

I put my hands up and backed away against every fiber in my body that screamed for me to get in the first strike and take the advantage in the fight. Jayce brushed past Brie and swung for my head. I ducked and instinct took over. I butted my head against his stomach and bowled him over. He grabbed my shoulders and pulled me over after him. I rolled over the top of his head and landed back on my feet in a crouch, then spun back to face him, my hands loose and muscles tense for his next attack. He pushed up to his feet and started toward me again.

"Jayce!" Nikko yelled from the door. He ran down and stood between us, a hand on Jayce's chest. "Jayce, think about what you're doing."

"I know what I'm doing," Jayce growled, his eyes locked on mine.

"No, you don't," Nikko said. He shoved Jayce hard enough to make him take a few steps back. "Look who you're attacking. Kale could tear you apart. It's what he's trained to do."

Jayce's chest rose and fell as he glared from Nikko to me. His eyes then widened slightly and he dropped his hands to his sides. "But the danger. You said so yourself they'd be on us in a heartbeat if they ever found out." He pointed at the pile of cloth he had thrown on the ground. "I found that on the bridge. What do you think they would do if they found you without it?"

"Who?" Brie demanded.

I looked at where Jayce pointed and recognized my crumpled trench coat. I walked over and picked it up, my eyes never leaving Jayce. "The police," I answered. I clenched the fabric hard in my fist. "You're right, Jayce. I put us all in danger."

"Kale, no," Brie protested.

I glanced at her. "He's right, Brie. It's too dangerous, and I know better. I just wasn't thinking."

"None of us are thinking too clearly after all the cramming for midterms," Nikko said in an urgent tone. "Let's get in the house and talk about this. There's no need to make any rash decisions."

I looked at Jayce and he nodded, his eyes on my wings. The shadow from the porch light behind me pooled at my feet, and I saw what he did. My wings were open, held out and loose, no longer bound tightly to my back. In my shadow, I looked like a huge winged beast waiting to spring.

I pulled my wings in tight and threw the coat around my shoulders as I walked up the porch steps behind Jayce. A slight shudder ran through me when the coat settled around my shoulders; it felt as though I relinquished my freedom with the simple action, but I pushed the feeling down and stepped into the house.

Chapter Seven

"It can't be like this, we all know it can't," Jayce said with a shake of his head.

"Then what does Kale have to do, leave?" Brie protested.

"Yes," Jayce and I said at the same time.

Jayce glanced at me. "It's not that I don't like you. I think you're great and all; it's just if they find you here-"

"I know." I stared out the living room window at the night beyond. "It'd be a danger to all of you."

"And yourself," he pointed out. "This area isn't exactly the safest place to hide from the cops if you know what I mean. They're always on the rounds here, checking for underage drinking parties and what not. It's only a matter of time."

"But we're not out of time yet," Nikko said. "We just need to be more careful."

"But you were meant to fly," Jayce replied. He met my gaze. "We might as well break your wings again; it's like you're being held hostage anyway. I know I'm not the only one who's noticed how often you stare out at the sky." He glanced meaningfully at the trench coat. "I can tell how much you hate wearing that thing."

"And where would you like him to go?" Brie asked. She sat in a corner of the couch with her knees drawn up under her chin and her hands clenched around them. "It's not like places are screaming welcome for Galdoni." She looked as though she was fighting back tears.

"I'll be fine," I told her. I couldn't bear to meet her gaze. Jayce's expression was firm, his fear for his sister in his eyes. Nikko's brow furrowed and I assumed he was searching for a way around the problem, a solution that would make everyone happy. I shook my head. "The plan was for me to go back to the Academy when I was healed, and I'm good enough now. I've got to stop what they're doing; it's wrong and there's got to be a way to end it."

"But putting yourself in danger isn't going to solve anything," Brie argued. "They're going to start the Arena battles again. What's to stop them from throwing you back in there?" I could hear the heartbreak in her voice and it tore through my chest like a dagger.

"That's what I've got to figure out," I replied quietly. "I'll go tonight."

"Tomorrow," Nikko said; his was voice firm. "There's no reason to leave right now. We'll all sleep on it and perhaps a better solution will present itself in the morning."

I met his gaze prepared to argue, then shrugged. "You know there won't be a better solution tomorrow. There's only one answer to this and it's the one we've known from the start." I put a hand briefly on his shoulder before I made my way past him to my room. "Thanks for trying, though."

I stopped at the door and turned back. "Jayce?" He looked up, his expression dark. "I'm truly sorry for putting Brie in danger. You know I never intended it."

"I know," he answered quietly.

I glanced at Brie and held her gaze for a second. Tears made her eyes shine bright; I cursed myself for making her cry twice in one night. I turned and shut the door behind me, then slid down against it until I sat on the floor, my wings to either side and my good knee under my chin. Darkness filled me so deep that it threatened to destroy any light I had found away from the Academy.

***

Someone banged on the door near my head and I jumped. It took me a second to remember why I was sitting on the floor, but the memories of merely a few hours earlier came rushing back all too quickly.

"What is it?" I forced out through a dry throat.

"Jayce and Brie need your help. Come quick." The urgency in Nikko's voice left no room for argument.

I pushed to my feet, wincing at the pain in my knee from sitting on the cold floor. My wings ached, but I ignored them and pulled the door open.

Jayce and Brie sat at the card table, their heads close together as they spoke in quiet undertones. Brie held a cellphone and when she looked up at me, her eyes were rimmed with red and her cheeks pale.

I took the chair across from her. "What's going on?"

"Our mom called," Jayce said. "She was hysterical. She said Rob got drunk and beat her, then went after Allie. She hasn't been able to find Allie anywhere."

Brie buried her face in Jayce's shoulder to hide her sobs.

"It's going to be okay," Nikko said. "They'll find her."

"Did he hurt her?" I demanded. Protectiveness, a feeling I had never known before, welled up in my chest at the thought that this Rob had hurt someone Brie and Jayce loved.

"We don't know," Brie said. "Rob's back home, but he doesn't remember anything, and I think he's still drunk by the sound of things."

"We're hoping she'll call. She knows the number," Jayce explained. Their eyes both turned back to the cellphone.

"How far away did you say it was?" I asked.

"Two hours," Nikko replied behind me. "But the buses don't run there until morning, and a cab would cost more than we've got. Their dad left on a training trip and won't be back for a couple days, and Dad's on an emergency call at the hospital."

The phone rang and Brie handed it to Jayce, her eyes wide with a mixture of hope and fear.

"Allie? Allie honey, where are you?"

Jayce's voice was calm, but his knuckles showed white where he gripped the phone. Brie hovered as close as she could to listen in.

"Okay, just stay there. We'll find a way to come get you. Can I talk to the manager?" He and Brie exchanged a worried look and she stepped back.

"Where is she?" Nikko asked.

"The video store down the road. Luckily, they're open twenty-four seven," Brie replied, her eyes on Jayce.

"Thank you. We'll be there as soon as possible. Bye." Jayce closed the cellphone with reluctance. "He said he'll watch over her until we show up. She sounds so scared."

"Rob better keep a safe distance when I see him again," Brie threatened, a dangerous spark in her eye.

"Okay then," Nikko cut in. "How are we going to get you guys there?"

"I'll take them," I said without hesitation.

Everyone turned to stare at me. Brie shook her head. "You can't fly with both of us and still get Allie. Besides, you've already flown too much today. You need to rest your wings or you'll seriously hurt yourself."

I shook my head. "I know I can make it, and you need someone there fast. You said yourself that the buses don't run 'til morning, you don't have a car, and I know you don't want to leave her there any longer than you have to." I frowned. "And you don't want to chance this Rob guy finding her. I don't see that you have many options other than to trust me."

Brie and Nikko both looked at Jayce. He studied me, his face pale and eyes calculating. "You think you can fly us both there?"

Nikko cleared his throat. "He might, but how would you all get home. One of you go, and since Brie's lighter, I suggest her. Give Kale the best possible chance to return."

Jayce stared at the wall behind Nikko and I could see him weighing the options. He finally sighed and turned back to me. "Fine. If you think you can do it, go for it. But if anything goes wrong, call me right away."

"Got it."

He glanced at Brie, then back. "And take care of my girls. If anything was to happen to them. . . ."

"Yeah, I remember," I said with a meaningful nod toward the front yard.

He gave a tight smile and slapped me on the shoulder. "Nice to see those wings are good for something."

I walked with Nikko to the front door to give the siblings some privacy before we left. Nikko took a deep breath of the cool night air. "You sure you can make it that far?" he asked, watching me out of the corner of his eye.

"There's only one way to find out."

He gave a short nod. "Right. I supposed so. Well, good luck. And thanks. That little girl means the world to all of us; I don't know what we'd do if anything happened to her."

I stood quietly for a moment. A strange sort of adrenaline filled me at the thought of the flight. I realized after a moment that it had even more to do with who we might meet at the end. My body yearned for a fight. I swallowed uneasily and voiced the thoughts in my head. "I can't promise to be rational if we meet up with this Rob guy. It's one thing to fight someone who's trained, but a little girl? It makes me so angry I can barely think. Nothing I've gone through has prepared me for this." I clenched and unclenched my fists in an effort to stay calm.

Nikko leaned against a post and studied me. "Just do what your conscience tells you. And remember that murder is illegal no matter who you are."

A humorless laugh escaped my lips. "Thanks, I'll try to remember that."

Brie opened the door and walked with me to the lawn. "Take care of her," Jayce said in a tight voice from the porch.

I nodded and wrapped my arms around her waist. "Ready?"

"Ready."

I stretched out my wings to ease the ache from our earlier flight, then gave three powerful downward thrusts. We lifted into the air and it took less than a second to clear the tree line. Brie held my arms, but her touch was soft. I followed her directions and winged toward the glow of another city on the dark horizon. I flew higher, then glided along the night wind in an effort to save my strength. The chill of the crisp air cut through us and Brie drew closer in my grasp. Her warmth kept me going.

We made it to the edge of the city within an hour by cutting straight across big chunks of forest where cars were forced to follow the meandering road. I landed as close to the video store as we dared, then slipped into the trench coat Brie had carried. She threw me one last worried look before running toward the store. I followed close behind, my senses straining for any sign of attack.

"Brie!" a young voice called out as she pulled open the door.

"Allie!"

I stepped inside and squinted in the neon light in time to see a little blond-haired girl throw her arms around Brie's waist. I caught the glimmer of tears in Brie's brown eyes as she knelt down and stroked the little girl's hair. "It's alright. We're going to take you with us."

"I was so scared," Allie sobbed. "He was so mean to Mom, and I told him to stop. Then he got really mad and I ran."

"He didn't hurt you?" Brie asked anxiously. Despite Allie's reassurances that she was alright, Brie held her back at arm's length and looked her over from head to toe. Satisfied, she pulled her back in for another hug. "I'm so glad you're safe."

"I'm glad you're here," Allie replied. She wiped her nose with the sleeve of her shirt, and I noticed a ragged teddy bear tucked under one arm. She glanced up at me and her eyes widened slightly.

"That's Kale. He's the one that got us here so fast." Brie glanced at me, then at the watching store manager. "Thank you so much. We really appreciate it," she told him.

"No problem. She was no trouble at all." We turned to leave and I could feel the manager's eyes on us as we made our way out the door into the night.

Brie knelt down on the sidewalk outside. "Allie, I think we need to go by the house and let Mom know you're okay."

"No!" Adrenaline rose in my veins at the terror in her voice.

"It's okay; you'll be safe. And you're coming back with us no matter what they say. But this way we can make sure Mom's okay, alright?"

Allie looked from Brie to me, her eyes on my face. "You're keeping us safe?"

I nodded in reply. She came over and took my hand. "Then we'd better stay close," she said quietly to her bear. A lump rose in my throat.

I looked at Brie; she gave me a small smile and turned to lead the way. Allie's little hand felt so light and fragile in mine; I was worried I would crush it. I kept my grip as loose as possible, then fought back a smile when she held on that much tighter.

We walked four blocks and then turned south into a cul-de-sac. A red car sat in front of a little gray house with light blue trim. "Looks like they're still home," Brie said quietly. We walked into the yard and she motioned for me to keep Allie on the grass.

At her knock, the door opened to reveal a woman in a night robe with disheveled brown hair. Bruises circled her eyes and her lip was swollen and split. I had to remember not to clench my hands. Allie's little one still held mine, and her grip tightened at the sound of a man's gruff voice.

"Who is it? Is it the cops? Have they brought her home?"

Brie's mom threw her arms around Brie and they embraced. "It's not the cops; it's Brie," she said over her shoulder.

"Brie? What the heck's Brie doing here? She should be at her dad's." The voice got louder. A tall man older than Brie's mother with black hair streaked in gray appeared at the door. He wore a blue football shirt and gray sweat pants. Allie let out a little squeak and scooted behind me.

"It's okay," I whispered. "I won't let him hurt you."

"Brie? What in the blazes-"

"Shut up, Rob. How dare you lay a finger on Mom? Look at her face. Look at what you've done!" Her mother touched her swollen cheek, but avoided looking at her husband. "We've got Allie and we're taking her away with us."

"Like heck you are!" Rob spat.

I took a step closer at the vehemence in his voice.

"We are, and there's nothing you can do about it unless you want me to call the police and let them settle it. They'd only need to take one look at Mom's face to slap you in jail again. Maybe they'll be smart about it this time and keep you there. How they ever let you guys keep custody of Allie is beyond me."

"Why I-," he lifted a hand.

"Stop right there." The growl in my voice carried across the lawn.

The three of them turned to look at me.

"Who's that?" Rob demanded.

Brie gave me a small smile. "My friend, Kale. He's helping me get Allie home for good and away from you." She glanced at her mom, and I caught the slight nod of agreement her mom gave her.

"What right does he have-"

"What right? You dare talk about rights the way you've treated everyone?" Brie yelled.

"You are not taking Allie, and that's final," Rob said; his eyes glittered with anger and a hint of drunkenness. He reached behind him through the door and brought something out. My heart slowed when I saw that it was a shotgun.

"Rob!" Brie's mom said in shock.

"Can you stay here and not make a sound?" I whispered to Allie, forcing my voice to remain calm despite the anger that welled in my chest. She nodded and I let go of her hand. She held her teddy bear tight and watched me with wide eyes.

I made my way slowly up the sidewalk, clenching my fists in an effort not to tear apart the man who threatened Brie.

"Now just hold it right there," Rob said, aiming the gun at my chest. I stopped a few feet away.

"Rob, no!" Brie protested.

He grinned. "You think you can just march in here and take my daughter-"

"She's not your daughter," Brie cut in, her voice tight.

Rob ignored her. "And I'm going to let you off without a fight?" He pursed his lips and his tone grew ugly. "What kind of man would I be if I let my daughter go off with a perfect stranger?"

I met his eyes. "A better man than one who beats his wife and scares little girls."

His eyes widened, then narrowed. His finger tightened on the trigger.

I leaped forward and grabbed the gun with my left hand before he could shoot, then I punched him with a right hook to the jaw hard enough to make him stagger against the door.

"I'll beat the living-"

I cut Rob's words off with another punch. His nose broke under my fist. He cupped his face, his nose streaming blood. I handed the gun to Brie and she took a few steps onto the grass with her mother.

"Why you-" Rob swung at me and I ducked, then bowled into his chest with my shoulder. The door opened behind him, sending us both sprawling onto the living room floor. Rob jumped up and tried to kick me in the groin, but I grabbed his foot and rolled on it, forcing him back to the floor to avoid a broken leg. He yelled and punched me in the ribs but I barely felt it past the rage that clouded my thoughts.

My instincts screamed for me to snap his neck and with each punch the feeling intensified. I stumbled back against the wall in an effort to control my anger. Rob picked up a lamp, throwing the lamp shade to the ground and ripping the cord from the wall.

"Didn't realize who you were up against, did you?" he said with a triumphant grin despite his bleeding nose.

He swung the lamp at me. I blocked it with my forearm and the bulb shattered. I punched him square in the face with my other hand. He stumbled back and dropped the lamp to clutch his bleeding nose again.

I turned back to the door and closed it before the others could come in.

Rob stumbled back against the couch, fumbling for a rag that lay on the ground beside a spilled can of beer. He pressed it against his face. "How dare you come into my home and take my daughter from me."

I could smell the liquor on his breath and fought to calm my pounding heart at the sight of the torn up house, broken lamps, pictures fallen off the walls, end tables upturned, and a hole through the television. The fear in Allie's voice echoed in my head, and it was all I could do to keep from knocking the man down again. I remembered Nikko's advice and took a deep breath.

"She's not your daughter, she's your step-daughter, and you've treated her as no child should ever be treated." I took a step closer to him despite the warning in my mind to stay as far away as possible to keep from killing him.

I slipped off my trench coat but kept my wings held tight to my back. "You've hurt people I care about, and I don't take kindly to grown men who beat up women and terrify children. There's not a place in this world for men like that." I walked toward him as I spoke, following him as he backed up around the couch.

"This is my house and that's my wife and daughter," he said in protest. At my glower, he leaned against a chair by the wall.

My hands ached to throttle him. "You might own a wooden frame and a few pieces of furniture, but you don't own anyone's life. You have no right to touch a hair on their heads with the intent to harm." I lifted my wings and he cowered back against the wall with a squeak of surprise. "Threaten or harm them again and it'll be the last thing you do. Understand?"

He nodded.

"Then say it," I growled.

"I un-understand," he stuttered, his eyes full of terror.

"Anyone you tell of this will think you're crazy. You don't want to go to a mental ward, do you?"

"N-no."

"Then this is between us. Take care of your loved ones or I'll take care of you." I tried to hide an amused smile at his speechless nod and tucked my wings back down. I took a deep breath and forced the anger away even though my instincts demanded for me to finish him. I slipped on the coat before I left through the door.

"Mrs. Ross," I said in passing with a nod of farewell. She stared at me, then glanced through the door.

"Let's go," I said in an undertone to Brie.

The sisters followed me down the driveway and across the gravel road to an orchard. After about ten minutes of silence, Brie hurried to catch up. "Did you kill him?" she asked in a whisper so Allie couldn't hear.

"Did you want me to?" I asked back. I fought to keep my tone carefully neutral. My heart tightened at the glance she threw me. "You expected me to." The realization felt like a knife through the tattered shreds of my heart. I clenched my teeth and strode faster, purposefully leaving them behind.

She thought I would kill him, and didn't protest when I went into the house and shut the door behind me. Was it because she was afraid of me, or because she felt Rob deserved it? It didn't matter. Either way, the fact that she thought I would kill an unarmed drunk man burned through my limbs with a fiery hatred for what I was. What was worse was how close I had come to giving in to my instincts and ripping his life away.

We walked away from the house into the sparse countryside lit by the first gray reaches of early dawn. I kept silent until I could control my emotions enough to face them. I avoided Brie's eyes and knelt to talk to Allie.

"We're going to go for a ride. Is that okay with you?" At Allie's nod, I shrugged off my coat. She shivered slightly in the cool air and I wrapped it around her shoulders. She gave me a small smile. "Don't be afraid," I said quietly. She nodded again.

Still kneeling, I opened my wings slowly to their full length. Allie stared at them for a second, then, to my surprise, she stepped closer and ran her fingers through the feathers. At her gentle touch, a shiver ran through me and she smiled. "I think you need the coat."

"I'm okay," I said past my tight throat. I opened an arm and she stepped underneath. I rose and motioned for Brie. "Ready?"

She nodded, her expression unreadable. I put an arm around her waist and beat my wings hard. We rose into the air, the weight heavier than I had expected after the long journey. I pushed harder and forced us high above the trees. We glided on the morning breeze, a dark speck above a waking countryside.

Allie shivered in the crisp air and curled against me. Eventually, I felt the steady rise and fall of her warm breath against my arm as she slept. Brie stayed silent, a fact for which I was grateful because it took all my concentration and waning strength to make it home.

Nikko and Jayce ran out when we landed just after sunrise behind Nikko's house. With a quiet thanks, Jayce took the sleeping girl from my arms and carried her to their home next door. Brie began to fill Nikko in on what had happened, so I left them and stumbled wearily into the house. I fell onto the couch with the intention of resting for a minute before making my way to the bedroom, but the cushions beckoned invitingly and I didn't have the strength left to protest.

Chapter Eight

I stared at the back of the Galdoni boy's head. He tried to throw an elbow in protest, but I tightened my hold around his neck and he froze.

"Well done, KL426," the passionless voice spoke above us. I looked up to see that the rest of the lunchroom had fallen silent. When I met his gaze, the guard gave a cold smile that didn't meet his eyes. "Now finish him."

Anger at what the boy had done still clenched in my gut, but I fought against it and shook my head.

"He stole your food, you won the fight; now finish him." The words were spoken as though they made perfect sense. Out of the corner of my eye, I saw older Galdoni push each other aside for a better view. The boy in my choke hold was older than me by three years. We had fought before, but something had brought out the rage in me tonight. He now held perfectly still even though I loosened my hold.

I shook my head again and dropped my arms. The boy fell to the floor, his brown wings ruffled and throat bright red. I could feel the claw marks from his fingers across my chest. He rolled over and looked at me. Our eyes met for the briefest second, his filled with relief, mine with trepidation.

"When are you going to learn, KL426? You don't let an enemy go." The onlookers scooted back a half second before the whip cut into my chest, carving a deep gash from my collarbone to the bottom of my ribs. I gasped and stumbled to my knees. The second lash wrapped around my neck and cut deep along my jaw. I ground my teeth and fought to stay silent. The older Galdoni boy sat still on the floor in front of me, too scared to move. He held my gaze in silence.

***

"Kale?"

I opened my eyes at the sound of the doctor's voice. Dr. Ray smiled at me from his seat near the table. "Yes, doctor?" I rubbed my pounding head and slowly sat up. My muscles protested and my stomach growled.

"You've been asleep for quite a while."

I glanced around and found the others watching me with concerned expressions. Allie sat on Brie's lap on the other couch and gave me a beaming smile. "You okay?" Brie asked, her brow creased.

I nodded, but it was hard to ignore the ache in my over-used wings. I glanced out the living room window and the sun setting beyond. "I slept the whole day?"

"Two days, in fact," the doctor replied with a humored smile.

"But school!" I stood up so fast my head spun and I had to reach for the table to keep from falling over. Jayce grabbed my arm to steady me.

"Whoa, there," he said. "You just wore yourself out, that's all. You can miss classes for a day or two."

"You would know," Nikko replied.

Jayce laughed, but he watched me with worried eyes. "You sure you're okay?"

I nodded, embarrassed at the attention. "I'm fine. I can't believe you guys let me sleep that long. And on the couch? What if someone walked in and found me here? Everyone would be in trouble."

Jayce shrugged. "So what? After what you did for us, we'd all go down fighting."

I stepped back from his grasp and stared at them. Everyone had the same expression, defiant and stubborn.

100

Even Dr. Ray met my gaze without flinching, though his jaw tightened slightly at my frown. "You can't do that." I gestured at the room. "You can't endanger what you have here because of me. It's not worth it."

"It is-" Brie stopped when I held up my hand.

I shook my head, exasperated. "It's not, and I don't know what to do about it."

"Nothing needs to be done," Jayce said with his own frown.

"I should go."

"No," Brie and Allie replied at the same time. The little girl stared at me with big brown eyes that matched her sister's. Her blond hair had been combed into two braids and hung from her shoulders, a bright counterpart to her red shirt. Innocence shone from her face and it was hard to look away.

"Going back now would defeat the purpose of hiding," Nikko argued. "We still have research to do."

I leaned back against the arm of the couch and glared at the floor. But Nikko was right. I took a deep breath and let it out slowly. "Alright." Out of the corner of my eye, I saw a smile pass between Brie and her brother. I gritted my teeth in frustration. "But we've got to be more careful. This isn't worth any of you getting thrown in jail, and your license taken away, Doc." I looked at him, but he merely shrugged.

Jayce threw himself on the couch. "Good, it's settled. Everything goes back to normal."

"Let's make dinner," Brie said to Allie.

I rubbed my eyes in an attempt to organize the thoughts swirling in my head.

"You did a good thing, Kale," Dr. Ray said gently, taking a seat next to Jayce on the couch.

"Surprised?" I asked.

He shook his head. "Relieved. I wish I had been here to get Allie myself. Kids should never be mixed up in a situation like that."

"We should have gotten her out of there sooner," Jayce said, his eyes full of regret. "Dad's planning to file for full custody so that she never has to go back."

"I don't get it," I admitted. "Why does your mother stay with Rob if he's abusive?"

Jayce shrugged, his expression sad. "That's what I'd like to know. But you can't reason with her. She loves Rob and he treats her well when he's not drunk."

"So he can beat her up and just apologize?" I stared at him.

Jayce shrugged again and studied his hands.

Dr. Ray gave me a thoughtful look and changed the subject. "How have you been doing having to stay in the house all day when you're not at school?"

I shrugged. "I get a bit restless," I admitted.

He pursed his lips, hesitated, then said, "What do you think about getting a job?"

I stared at him; Nikko and Jayce did too.

"A job doing what?" Jayce asked with a laugh. "And why?"

"He wants the complete human experience, so why not let him have it?" the doctor asked.

Nikko watched us both quietly.

"Somebody's paying for my food, and I know money's not easy to come by, so why not?" It made sense the more I thought about it. "I don't have any qualifications, so I'll probably have to work in fast food or something to start." The thought made me smile.

Dr. Ray replied with an answering grin, "I don't think you could hide those wings under a uniform."

"Yeah," Jayce piped in. "And I'm sure the laws about animals in restaurants'll put a damper on your interviews."

"Hey!" I said and he chuckled.

Nikko gave a thoughtful frown. "You know, they do need someone for security at the city center since they let Bode go for spray-painting the library."

"He must have had an overdue book he didn't want to pay for," Jayce replied. He laughed at his own joke.

Dr. Ray groaned. Nikko rolled his eyes and turned back to me. "But the job would be perfect. It's night patrol, and you could wear your coat. Plus, it's only a few blocks from here, so you could walk."

It actually sounded promising. "I'd just walk around and keep things safe?"

"Exactly. I doubt they've filled it yet and you're more than qualified to handle a few drunks wandering the grounds at night."

Dr. Ray nodded. "I'm on the city council. It shouldn't be too hard to get you on. I'll talk to Mr. Mason at the security office. I'm sure we can swing something."

"Perfect." My stomach growled and I gave a half smile. "Did someone mention dinner?"

Allie giggled from the doorway. Nikko and the doctor left to the kitchen to help; my body still ached with exhaustion, so I sat on the couch by Jayce.

After a few minutes of staring at the ceiling, he turned to me with a slightly annoyed expression. "What'd you have to go and do that for?"

Surprised, I stared at him. "What?"

He looked up at the ceiling again in mock despair. "Why me?" He turned back to me and rolled his eyes. "Being so gung-ho to get a job. You're making me look bad!"

I fought back a grin. "I'm indebted to all of you. You've kept my secret; it's the least I could do. Besides, I've never had a job. It sounds like fun."

Jayce shook his head and settled more comfortably on the couch. "You don't owe us anything. You brought Brie and Allie back safe. That's more payment than all the money in the world." He glanced up and I followed his gaze. Allie peeked at us from the kitchen door. I smiled and she jumped back out of sight. Jayce nodded again. "More than enough. If you want a job for the heck of it, go ahead. But remember, you've paid whatever dues you feel you owe here."

The thought made me smile. "Thanks."

He pushed up from the couch and slapped my shoulder as he went by. "Don't mention it." He paused. "And the less you talk about the job, the better for all of us. Me specifically."

I laughed and he disappeared toward the scent of food.

***

At dinner I caught Brie looking my way, but whenever I met her eyes she dropped her gaze with a flush of embarrassment. My thoughts were tangled after the bridge and then rescuing Allie. I couldn't fight the heaviness in the pit of my stomach when I thought of the look on Brie's face when I realized she expected me to kill her step-father.

I took a breath to calm my thoughts, then called her name before she could leave with everyone else after dinner was over.

She glanced at Allie who sat on the couch with a pink stuffed animal puppy which she was wrapping in different rags from the kitchen. Brie turned back to me and her voice quivered. "Kale, I'm so sorry."

The tears began to spill down her cheeks and I forgot what I was going to say. I fought down the urge to dry her cheeks with my fingers. "Brie, you don't have to cry."

She nodded and, wiping at her tears, pulled a chair close and sat so that our knees touched. "Yes I do. I was wrong about you, terribly wrong. I didn't mean to hurt you."

I whispered the truth that pounded with my heartbeat, "You could never hurt me."

She met my eyes and hope and pain warred on her face. "How could you forgive me? I thought you would kill him. I thought-"

"That killing my enemies is so ingrained into who I am that I couldn't control it?" I finished.

She dropped her eyes and looked away. "I'm sorry," she whispered.

I shook my head and touched her hand. "You saved my life, Brie. You helped me start over when I thought it wasn't possible. You believed in me." She looked away but I brushed her fingers with my own. "You make me better just by daring to be near me."

She looked back at me and the shadow of a smile touched her lips. "You're an amazing guy," she said quietly. She wrapped me in a hug and buried her face against my chest.

I ran a hand down her soft hair and closed my eyes, taking in the scent of her flowery perfume. My heart pounded and I wondered if she heard it. When she finally sat back up, her face glowed despite the tear tracks down her cheeks. I wiped them gently away with the backs of my fingers and she smiled a soft smile that warmed my soul.

***

"You're the new kid Dr. Ray sent over?"

I fought down a sudden rush of nerves and nodded.

The man behind the desk glanced at the papers in front of him. He was a head shorter than me but was stout and solid in the shoulders. He wore a red hat with thick brown hair poking out around the edges and had a nose that looked like it had been broken more than once. His hands were strong with thick, beefy fingers, and he twirled a nightstick as he read through the papers like he knew how to use it.

"Says here you're from California?"

I nodded. "Dr. Ray's my uncle. I'm staying with him to finish up the school year while my dad looks for work." The story Dr. Ray had come up with sounded false to my ears; I hoped Mr. Mason didn't catch it.

"Times are tough," he said with an understanding nod.

I waited silently and watched his eyes run down the paper, my heart pounding in my chest.

"Says here you're proficient in martial arts." He glanced up at me again. "We let the cops handle the major stuff, but it's good if you can take care of yourself in sticky situations."

I nodded and fought back a wry smile. "I can take care of myself."

He finished reviewing the résumé, then set it on his desk and rose to his feet. "I'll give you a two-week trial; if things work out, you have a job." He held out his hand.

A feeling of relief washed through me and I stood and shook his hand. "Thank you, sir. I won't let you down."

He gave me a thoughtful look. "No, I don't think you will." He held out the nightstick he had been twirling along with a flashlight and a utility belt. "Put these on and I'll show you around."

107

I followed him through the city grounds, enjoying the easy familiarity he had with the buildings. He showed me a few tricks, like where to look for students who wanted to hide out and party, which locks were the most often picked, and where a family of raccoons had made their home in the hollow of a tree near the old city building. He tossed a few pieces of dried bread on the ground at the foot of the tree and winked at me when a pair of eyes peeked out, shining in the setting sunlight.

I appreciated the amiable silence while we walked the beat. When we made it back to the main building, he tossed me a spare set of keys to the grounds. "Good to have you with us, son."

***

Moonlight lit the grounds in a peaceful glow, illuminating the buildings that lined the sidewalks like watchful sentries. It was my third night of the watch; I had one more tomorrow, then three off with the rotating schedule. I truly enjoyed security duty. Walking the city center grounds at night was like watching ghosts of the day's commotion dance themselves out through the shadows. I imagined I could still hear the laughter and conversations that bounced between the great halls at noon, and see the students sprawled out studying and families eating picnics on the lawns. I wondered if the Arena echoed in the same way with the cries of the dying; the thought made me somber.

The city center was made up of the new city building, the new library, an old mill building that had been converted into a museum, a handful of smaller buildings grouped in one corner and preserved as the first settlers' dwellings, the old, towering city building for which the demolition plans kept getting pushed back, and a three-story parking garage. It was a good-sized beat checking doors and making sure no one was using the parking garage to make out, and I enjoyed the solitary time to remind myself what I was here for and to try to figure out a plan to stop the Arena battles.

I turned the corner of the library in time to hear a panicked shriek.

"Stop, please!" The cry came from the direction of the parking garage.

Memories flashed through my mind of brown and white feathers drifting toward dirty cement. I put a hand against the cool brick to steady myself. Healed wounds ached with the surge of adrenaline that filled my body. I squeezed my eyes shut in an attempt to close it out, but the cry sounded again, filled with terror this time.

"No, don't!"

I shook my head to clear it, reminding myself that this was a job and I was in charge. I pushed off from the wall. Following the sounds, I ran around the corner, through the alley between the city building and the old mill, and up the ramp to the top level of the parking garage.

A lone truck sat in the garage just out of reach of the lamp light. I crept through the dark around the edge of the lot to the source of the commotion.

Two young men I recognized as seniors from the high school had a girl pinned in the bed of the truck. Another student jumped up into the truck beside her. "Hold still, honey. We're just havin' a bit of fun."

The other two students laughed drunkenly.

"Let me go, Bryce. This isn't funny." She struggled and their grips tightened around her arms. "You're hurting me!"

"Then stop struggling." Bryce reached down to caress her face and she turned away from his touch. His jaw clenched in anger and he grabbed her hair.

Fire filled my veins along with the frustrated fury of that night not so long ago when I had almost died saving another. I stepped into the circle of light. "Let her go."

The two students dropped her arms and backed up in surprise. Bryce whirled and glared at me, his eyes flashing with anger. "Get out of here." He glanced at my nightstick and flashlight and gave a mocking smile, "Security."

"Leave her alone," I growled.

The girl backed up in the bed of the truck until she huddled in a corner near the cab. Bryce looked at her and a dark chuckle escaped his lips. "You want in on this too, hot shot?" he asked. He gave me a knowing smile.

Bile rose in my throat. "I don't want in on anything. I want her out of it and you three miles from here before the cops show up."

Bryce's chuckle turned into a growl. "What are you gonna do, tell on us? Cry to the police like a little girl? You security guards can't stop us anyway. You're supposed to report it and let the cops deal with it." He said the last sentence in a whiny sing-song tone that made my hair stand on end. He leered down at me from the bed of the truck, confident in his superior position.

By that time I had reached the truck. Rage filled my chest and I couldn't control it any longer. I reached over the lowered tailgate and grabbed him just above the knees.

He cried out in surprise and made a lunge for the side of the truck but I threw him with a twist of my shoulders. He flew over the side and landed on the pavement with a thud.

"What the?" one of the other students said in surprise.

I levered myself up into the bed of the truck and they backed up near the girl. "Get on the ground."

"Okay," the one on the right squeaked before he scrambled down the side and backed up near Bryce.

The second man took a step forward, his knees bent. "You don't know who you're messing with."

A surge of vicious glee rose in my chest. "You don't either."

He lunged, attempting to catch me off guard.

His shoulder caught me high in the chest, but I had already sized him up and knew my center of balance was lower than his. I grunted with the blow, and he barely moved me back inches. He slugged at my stomach and I rolled to the left, pulling his fist along. The force of both our efforts threw us off and we fell over the side of the truck.

I rolled when I hit the ground and came up with fists raised in time to block my own nightstick levered by Bryce. I threw it to the side, jabbed under his raised arm and felt his ribs give, then caught him across the jaw with a quick left.

Bryce stumbled back, the nightstick discarded between us. Footsteps announced an attacker behind me, and a spin kick sent the first man who had jumped out of the truck crashing back into its side. He crumpled to the ground with a whimper.

The third student let out an angry growl. He dove at me with his arms out like a linebacker attempting to drive his opponent into the ground. I moved to the side at the last second and elbowed him in the back with a simultaneous chop to the back of the head. My foot caught his leg and he landed with a thud on the pavement. He pushed up to his hands and knees and stared at the ground like he wondered what had hit him. It would be so simple to crush his windpipe or snap his neck. I had to fight the urge to eliminate him as a threat. I shook my head to clear it of the violent desires.

I backed up so the truck was behind me and glared at them. "As much as I'm enjoying this, I wasn't lying about the cops. They should be here soon and I'm guessing you won't want to be."

"Who are you?" Bryce growled, a hand clutched to his ribs.

"Kale, Security Guard."

He glared at me. "You'll pay for this."

"I look forward to it," I replied. I backed around the truck, careful to keep them all in sight. I offered the girl a hand. "Let's get you out of here."

She glanced back at Bryce, who glared at her and wiped a trickle of blood from his lip. She took my hand and I lifted her over the side of the truck. I watched Bryce and the other guy help their friend into the vehicle.

"You're not worth it, Krissy," Bryce spat out. "You were barely worth it when it was easy." Her hand tightened on my arm, but Bryce merely spit on the ground and climbed into his truck. We backed up and his tires squealed, leaving black rubber on the pavement as they sped away.

I watched them to make sure Bryce didn't have any sudden, vengeful feelings about running us down. He left the parking lot and squealed around the next corner and out of sight. It was then that I felt her hand tremble. I turned and saw that the girl had tears running down her cheeks.

"You okay?"

She took a deep breath and nodded, but I suspected that she kept holding my arm for more than just nerves. "Do you want to sit down for a minute?"

Her eyes widened and she dropped her hand. I knew she second-guessed my intentions and shook my head. "I really will call the cops if you'd like. I probably should anyway. Protocol and all. I just-"

She shook her head quickly. "No, please. They're gone and I'm okay. I don't want to make an uproar." She brushed her disheveled blond hair back from her face and straightened her shirt without looking at me.

"Okay. Then let me at least walk you home. I don't want Bryce getting any ideas."

She studied me for a minute before nodding. "Thank you. I don't live far from here."

"I'm Kale, by the way."

"Kristina," she replied with a small sniff. "But everyone calls me Krissy."

"Well, Krissy, let's get you home safe."

I offered her my arm and she took it again. I picked up my flashlight and night stick, and we walked quietly down the ramp to the street.

"You're new here?" she asked. "I haven't seen you around before."

I realized she was trying to keep her thoughts off of what had just happened. "Visiting," I answered, hoping it didn't sound forced. "I'm staying with Nikko Ray."

She gave a small smile. "He's Dr. Ray's son. Dr. Ray teaches my anatomy class. He's great." Her voice tightened. "Bryce and I signed up for the class together, but then he dropped it for P.E. because his grades were too low." She fell silent again.

"You're a brave girl," I said quietly. Our footsteps echoed against the houses on either side of the road. "You don't deserve to be treated that way. No one does."

"Bryce isn't usually like that." Her voice quivered. "He gets around his friends and he has to be all macho."

I frowned. "That wasn't macho. That would have been-"

She stopped walking and cut me off with a hand on my arm. "Don't say it." Tears trickled down her cheeks. "Bryce isn't a bad guy, but I don't know what would have happened if you hadn't shown up."

She shook like a leaf. I lifted a hand to comfort her and she leaned against my chest and cried. I froze, uncertain what to do. I patted her on the back tentatively. "He's gone. He won't hurt you anymore."

"Hey, get away from my sister!" The angry shout from a porch made us both turn.

"Zach, I-" Krissy started to explain.

I turned at the sound of a shoe on gravel behind us in time to avoid a haymaker to the head. I pushed Krissy behind me for protection. The adrenaline that had finally faded from the previous fight rushed through my bloodstream. I landed a straight jab to the attacker's mouth, splitting my knuckles open on his teeth. I slugged him in the stomach, then elbowed him in the back when he doubled over.

Two more young men came from either side. A roar filled my ears and at that moment, I wanted to hit someone, anyone, more than I ever had in my life. I had been trained for this, and my body relished the chance to finally lash out.

"Zach, no! Leave him alone!" Krissy yelled, her voice hysterical.

I ducked under another punch, then swung again but barely missed the guy. The other man kicked at my stomach. I blocked the kick with my forearms and grabbed his knee. I took out his other foot with a spin kick and he fell to the ground. A painful grunt escaped his lips.

"You'll pay for hurting my sister," Zach growled. I watched him out of the corner of my eye as I faced the last guy standing. Zach strode down the porch steps past Krissy.

She grabbed his arm. "He didn't hurt me. He saved me from Bryce."

"Bryce!"

I stepped in boxer-style and landed a straight punch squarely on the other man's jaw. He stumbled back and fell to his knees. I took a step forward and grabbed his throat with one hand. I could feel his pulse under my fingers. The roar grew louder, urging for me to finish him. I started to squeeze.

Zach ran at me from the side. I let go and hit Krissy's brother with a two-handed open palm blow to the chest that carried the force of my rage combined with his own momentum. The breath left his body in an audible whoosh as he fell backward to the grass, stunned.

I stepped forward to finish him with a straight punch, crushing his nose into his skull like I had been trained; he backed up on his elbows, his eyes wide. Red filled my vision, then Krissy grabbed my arm. "Kale, don't hurt him!"

The roar disappeared at her touch. I stared from her to Zach, my breath ragged in my throat. I couldn't believe what I had almost done, what every fiber of my being had urged for me to do.

"Kale, I-"

I shook my head. I couldn't speak. I stumbled past her onto the road. I looked back once at the four young men groaning in various positions on the grass, then turned and walked away.

"Krissy, he could have killed me," I heard Zach say, his voice shaking.

"He saved me. Bryce would have raped me," Krissy replied, her own voice trembling.

I turned a corner and disappeared into the welcoming darkness of the trees that lined the side of the road.

Chapter Nine

I stared at my hands. Blood flowed from the gash across my knuckles. They ached, wanting to hit someone again, to cause pain, to crush a windpipe and feel the pulse fade away.

A growl escaped my lips; I turned and punched a tree. The pain jolted away some of the bloodlust that filled me like oxygen. I hit the tree again, harder this time.

I didn't ask to be this way, and had pretended fairly well up to this point that I wasn't a killer, wasn't raised to be merciless and uncaring, to thrive on weaker flesh. I thought I had beaten them, that I could use logic to fight down the reflexes that had been ingrained into my body from the day I was born.

I stared at the red knuckles, and traced the flow of blood through my veins with my eyes. Who was I fooling? I wasn't born. I had been created in some test tube by sterile, cold-hearted lab technicians determined to make the perfect gladiator for money-hungry politicians. My bloodlust originally belonged to them.

I stumbled through the trees and began to run from my own existence. Tree branches and shrubs caught at my coat, but I didn't slow until I finally tripped on a root hidden in the shadow of night. I rolled with the impact and landed against an ancient pine. Breath tore raggedly through my throat. My vision cleared and I stared through the boughs to the star-scattered sky. I shouldn't be here, free, away from the Arena. No one was safe with me on the loose. The ache in my battered hands reminded me that I would never truly be free. They had a firmer grasp on me than I could have imagined.

I pushed back to my feet and walked slowly this time, not paying attention to where my feet were taking me until I stopped behind Nikko's house, the place that was the closest thing to a home I had ever had.

The backyard was dark, untouched by the few street lamps along the road in front of the house. I almost turned away, but movement in the back window caught my eye. Brie was speaking to someone out of sight. She gestured with a smile, her profile lit in a warm glow.

How could I even be around her? I was a genetically created killer. Why did she tolerate me? Why did any of them? Dr. Ray had been right in the beginning. I was a danger to them all.

My hands throbbed. I glanced at them. Something warm slid down my face. I raised a hand to my cheek and touched the last thing I expected. A tear. The first tear I had ever cried.

I stared at the shine of moisture on my fingers. It caught the starlight like a diamond, reflecting light the way I felt my soul reflect the darkness that had been nurtured there from a life of violence. Another tear fell onto my hand and cut a track through the blood. I wondered if anything could do the same for my soul. I gritted my teeth and brushed away the tears, angry at my hope that I could change, proving once again how futile it was to count on the intangible. I knew I was a danger to all in that house, and wondered why I didn't just leave.

I glanced up at the house and my heart slowed. Brie was looking out the window in my direction. I knew she couldn't see me standing in the night against the dark trees, but a jolt went through my body as though she stared into my soul. She laid me bare as no one else had ever done. My heart ached. At that moment I wanted to be human more than I ever had before.

And I knew why I stayed.

She took a step closer and touched the window gently. "Kale?" she mouthed.

I stepped back into the forest, my heart pounding. I heard the back door open and circled through the trees to the front of the house before I could hear her call my name and was forced to decide whether or not to answer.

I opened the front door and found Jayce in the living room. He looked down at my hands and his eyes widened. "Man, what happened to you?"

I glanced down at them also and frowned past the jumble of thoughts swirling in my head. "I stopped a rape."

"Geesh, how many of them were there? Thirty?" Jayce turned toward the kitchen. "Nikko, get in here. Kale needs your expertise."

"Kale?" Brie followed Nikko out of the kitchen, her tone confused. "But I thought. . . ." She glanced toward the kitchen window and her voice faded away as though she realized how strange it would sound.

"What?" Jayce asked, his attention on my hands as Nikko examined them.

"Never mind," Brie said, but her eyes held mine questioningly.

I looked away and pretended to care about my throbbing knuckles. I didn't know how to explain to her that I had almost killed someone, that I had almost become the person she thought I was when I stopped her step-father. I pushed down the feelings of guilt and turned my attention to Nikko as he checked the wounds.

Allie's blond-framed face appeared in the kitchen doorway, her eyes wide.

"Allie, please go home and play. Dad should be back soon," Brie urged her. "You don't want to see this."

"Is Kale okay?" she asked, her brown eyes wide with concern.

I nodded and she smiled, then skipped around us and out the front door. Brie watched to make sure she made it safely inside their house before closing the door again.

"You stopped a rape?" Nikko asked. He made me flex my fingers as he gently probed the torn flesh. "What did this?" He pointed to the gash across the right knuckles.

"Teeth," I replied.

Nikko probed the other hand. "And this?"

I met his eyes. "A tree."

Jayce's eyes widened and he looked from me to Nikko. But Nikko merely nodded and went to get his father's bag. "That first one'll probably need stitches. We might have to wait for Dad," he replied when he came back.

"It's fine, just bandage it."

He glanced up. "It'll scar if it's not stitched."

A laugh escaped me at the thought. "And you think that bothers me?"

He met my eyes, his expression calculating. I returned his gaze and after a moment, he gave a wry smile. "I guess not. Very well, as you wish." He opened his bag and took out some antibiotic ointment, gauze, and bandages.

"So what happened?" Jayce blurted out as though he couldn't hold it in any longer.

I glanced at Brie but couldn't read her expression. I dropped my eyes to the floor and forced my tone to be casual. "I was walking the second beat and had just finished at the library when I heard someone scream."

"Oh," Jayce interrupted, his eyebrows raised. "A damsel in distress."

Brie slapped his arm. "Quiet."

I gave her a smile of thanks. "I ran to the parking garage and found three guys in the bed of a truck with a girl." Nikko's bandaging slowed, but he kept his attention on my hands.

I closed my eyes and saw the fear on her face again; the same fear had echoed on her brother's face when he realized I could kill him.

"What did you do?"

Jayce's voice brought me back to the present. I shook my head to clear it and opened my eyes. "I convinced them that they should leave her alone."

Jayce slapped Nikko's shoulder. Nikko grunted as he tied off the last bandage. "Did you hear that Nik? He *convinced* them. I wish I would have been there to see that!"

I stared at him in amazement. If only he knew. He met my gaze and his grin faltered slightly.

A knock sounded at the door and I jumped up, still on edge.

"Steady Kale," Nikko said in a calming voice. "It's probably someone for Dad." Brie stood beside me and put a hand on my shoulder. Her touch slowed my pounding heart.

Nikko answered the door. Muffled voices came from the porch. Jayce stepped up next to him, blocking my view. I took a step back toward the bedroom in case I needed to vanish. Instead, Jayce pushed the door open wide. "Uh, Kale? You have visitors."

To my surprise, Krissy's brother Zach and his three friends from earlier crossed into the small living room. Heat rushed through my body and I clenched my fists. The bite of the bandages into my sore knuckles kept me grounded.

Nikko took a step to position himself between us. I stared at him in shock. No one had ever stood in harm's way for me before.

Zach lifted his hands. "We don't want trouble. We came to apologize."

Nikko glanced back at me, his eyebrows lifted. He must have seen the same astonishment on my face because he gave a slight shrug and stepped aside.

Zach walked to the couch. "Krissy told us everything. I owe you the world, man. We were stupid." He held out a hand. "I owe you her life and mine. Please accept my apology."

Instinct screamed that it was a trap, that he would pull me close and shove a concealed blade in my gut like any trained Galdoni; but I heard the sincerity in his voice and logic battled against instinct. Zach's hand lowered a fraction at my hesitation.

I took a deep breath to calm my nerves and accepted the handshake. "You thought I hurt your sister. You were being a good brother."

He grinned in relief. "I try, but it's nice to have someone I can count on when I'm not there." He glanced down at the bandages on my hand. "Rory said you knocked him pretty good."

He glanced back at the one I had hit in the teeth. Rory smiled good-naturedly, his teeth still red from bleeding gums. "You almost knocked my head off. I'm just glad my teeth stayed in my head instead of in your hand."

"Me, too," I agreed whole-heartedly.

"Where'd you learn to fight like that!" the one I had almost choked to death asked, rubbing his throat.

I shrugged uncomfortably. "My dad was big into martial arts."

"I've never seen anything like that," he exclaimed.

Zach leaned against the couch. "As a thank you, I wanted to invite you and your friends to a party we're having at my

122

house Friday night. My parents are out of town and it's gonna be wild. Do you work that night?"

My stomach tightened, but I shook my head. "No, not Friday."

"Great, we'll see you there!" Zach said confidently. He pushed off the couch and slapped Jayce on the shoulder on his way out the door, his friends close behind. Jayce shoved the door shut behind them and we all stared at it.

Jayce finally broke the silence. "Zachary Finch, the star quarterback of the football team, is the brother of the girl you saved from being raped?" The shock in his voice was echoed on Brie and Nikko's faces.

"I almost killed them," I forced out, my throat tight.

"I'll bet you did!" Jayce exclaimed.

I shook my head. "I almost killed them," I repeated, meeting his gaze. His eyes widened and his grin faded as the implication of my words sunk in.

"The red marks on the last guy's neck. You did that?" Nikko asked in a carefully neutral tone.

I felt the pulse under my fingers again, the rage screaming through my body for me to end it. I turned away from them and rubbed my hand on my leg in an effort to erase the feeling. A shudder ran through my body.

Nikko set a hand on my shoulder. "I think you should go to the party Friday."

I stared at him. "Are you crazy? Do you understand what I could have done?"

He nodded, his eyes searching mine. There wasn't any judgment on his face; instead, I found something I wasn't prepared to handle, understanding. "You need more social interactions that don't end in you fighting for your life. If killing and defending are all you know, then of course that's what you resort to. It's ingrained. You need to replace it with

123

something else or it'll never go away." He glanced at Jayce for concurrence.

Jayce nodded. He leaned against the door. "He has a point, Kale. So far, school and this place are all you know. It couldn't hurt to relax a bit."

"Couldn't hurt?" I repeated, appalled. "It could hurt, and it would most definitely be someone besides me. I'm dangerous, remember? I think the fewer social situations at this point the better."

"I think you should go."

We all turned to Brie in surprise.

"What?" I asked, not bothering to hide my shock.

"You should go. It might be the only chance you have to just chill with friends and have a good time."

"We have a good time here," I pointed out.

"That's different, and you know it," she argued. "What are you afraid of?"

My mouth dropped open as I searched for words. "Well, I. . . ." I sputtered and she gave me a small smile that made her brown eyes glow. I let out a sigh and told her the truth despite what she would think of me. "I'm afraid of killing or hurting someone by accident because it's so easy." I gestured vaguely at the door. "That would have been so easy, and that's what scares me. I didn't feel anything during the fight."

"But you do now," Nikko pointed out gently.

I rubbed my eyes with my palms in frustration. "Yes, I do."

"Then that makes you human," he concluded.

The energy left my body; I felt like a boxer who had just been punched in the stomach. I looked from him to Brie and Jayce and then back. They watched me with encouraging expressions, a tiny army banded together to fight my battle. I bit back the arguments that fought to get free and turned to my bedroom. "I'm not human," I said before shutting them out.

I didn't bother to turn on the light. The faint outline of the familiar furniture beckoned to me. I threw off my coat and settled onto the bed, the brush of dark feathers against the backs of my arms a reminder of what I would never be.

Chapter Ten

I followed Nikko and Jayce up the steps of Zach's house. "I don't know why I let you talk me into this," I said.

"Just relax; you'll have a good time," Brie insisted. She took my arm and walked with me to the open door where music and laughter spilled out like raucous sunlight after a storm.

Students filled every possible space, eating in the kitchen, playing pool on a scratched pool table in the back room, lounging on couches that looked like they had survived the last war, sitting on orange boxes turned into chairs, and in the back yard playing what appeared to be volleyball over a rope strung between two trees. Everywhere I looked, students laughed, ate, talked, drank, and danced to the thump of music coming from a rigged stereo in a corner by the pool table. Discordant music also came from two cars parked outside, the owners of which seemed to be trying to blast each other away through sheer volume.

Luckily it was cloudy outside and the air carried a touch of chill, so my coat wasn't out of place. I noticed several students sporting similar styles lounging on the lawn.

"Hey, you came!" Zach shouldered his way past a group of students by the door and met us on the porch.

"Yeah," I replied noncommittally, a bit overwhelmed.

"This is awesome!" Jayce said. With a wave in my direction, he and Nikko lost themselves in the crowd.

"I'm glad you made it," Zach said sincerely.

I took a calming breath. "Thank you. Where's Krissy? Is she okay?"

"She's fine, thanks to you. She went with my parents to my grandma's house for the weekend to kind-of get past everything. She didn't want me to tell our parents what

126

happened, but I'm hoping she'll do it while they're gone. That way my dad won't be able to kill Bryce at least until they get back," he said with a glint in his eye that said he thought Bryce deserved anything his dad would do.

I thought of what I had wanted to do and figured he would be better off with Krissy's dad. "Good idea."

Rory, the one I had almost strangled, made his way through the crowd to Zach's side. He smiled at Brie and my heart gave a strange thump. I stepped closer to her.

"Can I take your coats?" Rory asked. He held his hand out to Brie.

"No," I replied stiffly. Brie elbowed me discreetly in the ribs and I winced. "I mean, no thank you."

Rory laughed. "No prob, bro! Food's in there and y'all have a good time!"

Zach gave him a good-natured shove and he stumbled back toward the kitchen. He gave us an apologetic smile. "Don't mind him; he's Texan." He laughed as though it was an inside joke. "Make yourselves at home. If you need anything, don't hesitate to ask."

"Thanks," Brie answered for both of us.

He left up the stairs and we made our way slowly through the crowded hallway. We arrived at a back room where Jayce was throwing darts with a girl in braids. Several onlookers laughed when his dart missed the board altogether and stuck in the wall at least a foot away.

"You okay?" Brie asked in my ear after a few minutes.

"Yeah," I replied.

"You sure?" She put a hand on my arm so I would look at her. "You've been awfully quiet since Rory tried to take my coat."

"I think I felt jealous," I admitted.

"And that surprises you?" Brie asked with a sweet laugh that drowned out the noise in the room.

I nodded. "I've never been jealous."

She thought about that for a moment and then gave me a small, sweet smile I had never seen before. It made my heart beat faster and warmth tingled in my fingers and toes. "What?" I asked.

"No one's ever been jealous about me before."

I studied her sincere brown eyes as she stared up at me. I had never noticed the gold band that surrounded her brown irises like the first light of the sun, or the freckles that lightly spotted her nose. "I couldn't help it."

She gave me that special smile again and was about to say something else when someone called my name. I turned to find Jayce at my elbow. "How about it?"

"How about what?"

"A game of darts. I'll play you."

I shook my head, but Brie pushed my shoulder gently. "Go for it; it's fun."

"It's not like he's much competition," one of the onlookers shouted. He laughed at his own joke and almost fell off his rickety box chair.

Brie tipped her chin. "Nikko will show you how to play."

Nikko pulled the darts from the board and surrounding wall. "You can't be any worse than Jayce."

"Hey!" Jayce protested.

Nikko slapped him on the shoulder on his way past. "At least I don't need to tell you to go easy on him." Several of the onlookers laughed.

Nikko handed me the first dart. "Okay, now the goal is to hit the red dot in the middle. Of course, Jayce's goal is just to hit the dart board."

"At least I can do this!" Jayce balanced a dart on the tip of his finger for a moment. A passerby bumped him and the dart fell into someone's cup. "Crap."

"Nice." Nikko gestured toward the board. "Go for it, Kale."

I held the dart near the point like I had seen Nikko do and launched it toward the board. It floated through the air and hit the dart board just inside the edge.

"Not bad!" Nikko said encouragingly. "Try another one."

I studied the dart for a second. The way it was weighted held some promise. I gripped it near the tip again, but this time flicked it underhand like a throwing knife.

The dart whizzed through the air and landed with a sharp thump in the second ring from the edge. I felt the surprised stares of several onlookers.

"Whoa," Nikko said.

"Dare you to try that again," Jayce challenged.

I shrugged and, more comfortable with the weight now, held the dart closer to the end and flicked it toward the board. The dart stuck in the ring that surrounded the red center.

Some of the onlookers clapped. "Dang," Jayce said with his customary grin. "You've gotta teach me that. Do it again." He handed me one of his darts.

I shook off whatever liquid coated it from the cup and flicked it toward the board. This time it hit the center. Nikko and Jayce cheered the loudest; a crowd began to form.

"Ten bucks says you can't do that again," Zach shouted from the door as Nikko gathered up the darts.

"That was a lucky shot," Jayce said with a taunting grin. "I call for a rematch."

Nikko handed the darts back to me and said under his breath, "Kick his butt, again."

I chuckled and turned to the board. I threw my three darts in quick succession; each landed in the red center circle with a satisfying thud. The crowd cheered. A feeling I had never experienced before swelled in my chest like a balloon and I couldn't help but smile.

Rory poked his head in the door. "Hey you guys, the Arena's back on and the first fight's just begun. I didn't even know they were starting it up again."

In that instant, the balloon vanished to leave a deeper void than before. I had hoped that somehow the Arena wouldn't start again, that someone would find a loophole that would bring the whole murderous gambling show down. If the show disappeared, there wouldn't be a reason for me to return to the Academy. Rory's words destroyed that hope, and I cursed myself for letting Dr. Ray's intangibles get to me.

The crowd around us trickled into the living room. I moved to follow them, but Brie grabbed my arm. I turned to see my friends watching me. "We don't have to see it," Brie said.

"It's not a pretty sight," Nikko agreed.

I shook my head. "I need to see it; I need to know what it's really like."

The three of them exchanged looks, but no one moved to stop me. I made my way down the hall and into the overcrowded living room where everyone gathered around a small television.

I found a spot close to the window and leaned against the wall. Nikko, Jayce, and Brie took places nearby. I glanced around and was surprised to see uncertain expressions on most faces. Apparently the Arena games weren't as welcome as I thought.

"Welcome to the return of the Galdoni Arena!" the announcer proclaimed in an overly loud voice. "We apologize for the slight setback earlier this year, but now we are back and better than ever!" The camera panned to a view of the Arena from the outside. I had to admit that it looked pretty amazing. The Arena was domed in reflective black with marble pillars around the outside. Flames rushed from the top of each pillar and flowed up silver paths to join at the peak in a bonfire that changed from red to green to blue and was mirrored on each facet of the black dome.

"Now, brought to you with ten additional camera angles and enhanced sound quality, I give you the Galdoni warriors!" Fake applause dubbed into the show sounded as the picture split to show two cages on the Arena floor.

My breath caught. I recognized the first Galdoni as the boy from the lunchroom so long ago, the one I had been whipped for not killing. He stood taller now, and clenched the mace in his hands like he knew how to use it. He glanced up at the Arena dome and flexed his brown-feathered wings. This was the first time either of them would fly without chains beside their time outside the Arena. I hoped they hadn't spent the last six months behind the Academy wall.

I had only seen the second Galdoni once or twice at the Academy. He passed a scimitar from one hand to the other and bounced on the balls of his bare feet. Both Galdoni wore battle armor that made them look more animal than man. The Galdoni from the lunchroom wore dark silver armor that outlined his bones as though they were on the outside of his body. The armor was plated and the seams slid smoothly together as he walked to create a fluid, skeleton effect. He wore a skull mask with serrated horns; dark red outlined his eye sockets.

The other Galdoni wore dark bronze armor worked to mirror the sinewy body of a panther. Clawed gauntlets covered his hands and feet, rippling muscles were detailed

131

along his back and chest, and his mask bore the snarling face of an attacking wildcat. Both of their armor covered their wings up to the joints, ending in wicked, serrated spikes that made for lethal weapons during flight or on the ground.

"AR527 squares against TI620 in this fight to the death." The announcer's voice dropped into a dubbed recording. "Remember audience, the Galdoni were bred for one thing and one thing only, to fight and to kill. As in all Arena battles, this fight is to the death. Parents are asked to take special consideration when allowing young children to watch as the following content will be graphic in nature."

"You don't get much more graphic," someone in the crowd said. Another student shoved him and a brief scuffle broke out.

Brie put a hand on my arm. "You sure you want to watch this?" she asked quietly.

I nodded. My gut clenched as the cages opened and the two Galdoni stepped out. The students around us fell silent.

"AR527 takes to the air. He circles the Arena, watching for an opening. TI620 follows his movements from the ground. AR527 dives; he veers off at the last moment, inches from the other Galdoni's blade, and throws his mace in a surprising attempt to catch TI620 off guard. It works; the mace slams into TI620's shoulder. That's gotta hurt!"

AR527 landed a few feet away, watching for an opening to get his weapon back. TI620 switched his scimitar to the other hand. It was the only sign he gave of the injured shoulder. Blood dripped from his armor, but he ran forward as though he wasn't wounded.

"TI620 lunges, fakes to the right, and catches AR527 with a quick backspin as he tries to pick up the mace. AR527 rolls away from the blow, but it's obvious his wing has taken a hit! It's a telling blow. This might be a short fight tonight folks."

AR527 tried to fly to escape the other Galdoni, but his brown wing hung limp. Blood flowed freely to the sand-covered ground as he dodged to the left to avoid another quick slice. My wings ached with remembered pain and I fought back a grimace.

The commentator's voice rose in pitch. "TI620 slices through AR527's other wing, leaving him flightless. AR527 stumbles back, but the other Galdoni follows. TI620 swings again, but he's too close; AR527 dives at him and they both fall backward. The sword is loose! Both Galdoni scramble for the blade!" His voice rose higher. "TI620 reaches it first, but AR527 knocks it from his hand with a quick kick. They both scramble through the sand. AR527's got the sword. He raises it. But wait! TI620 has the mace!"

A few students in the crowd behind me cheered.

The announcer continued, "Where did that come from? Before AR527 can regain his footing, TI620 throws the mace; it hits the other Galdoni in the stomach just below his armor! He's down. TI620 rips the blade away and shoves it into AR527's throat!"

The Galdoni struggled against the blood-covered sword, but TI620 held him down with one hand. The gray-winged Galdoni picked up the mace and, still holding AR527 down with the blade, swung the mace at his head.

I heard a couple of groans and one cheer at the death blow, but when I looked around the room, the majority of the students stared somberly at the television. Two students near the door exchanged cash; I assumed the one on the receiving end was the guy who had cheered. A girl next to him shook her head and walked away.

"I can't believe dog fighting's illegal but this is considered legit." Zach turned off the television with a shake of his head.

133

"Just wait 'til they create genetically enhanced dogs," Jayce replied, his expression tight.

"What do you mean?" Rory asked.

Jayce glanced at me out of the corner of his eye. "That's how they justify it. Galdoni belong to the government, a product of our taxes and a major defense experiment gone wrong. Because they're 'government property'," he supplied the quotes with his fingers, "the government feels free to use them however they'd like. And the gambling tax creates a return on the investment, the government's way of erasing the mistake. The people've fallen for it. Except for the picketers outside the Academy gates, nobody's created much of a stir."

"Not that it would do anything," Zach replied. He looked directly at me, his expression frank. "What they do to the Galdoni is wrong and there's got to be a way to stop it." I met his gaze, surprised.

"The Galdoni are the ones doing it. Nobody says they have to fight." A black-haired boy I recognized from History argued. Zach gave me a small half-smile before he turned away.

"They're bred to fight," one of the guys in the back who had been part of the money exchange said. "It's what they are, remember? They're killing machines."

A girl threw a cup at him. "That's just how you justify it, Troy. You're holding blood money."

"Oh, yeah?" He said something in retort but I didn't hear it.

Most of the crowd had begun to dissipate, several through the front door and the rest back to their various activities. I followed a group to the back door and leaned against the porch railing as they picked up the volleyball and began to toss it around. A hand touched my arm. I turned to find Brie leaning against the railing next to me.

"I don't know what to say," she said in a soft, sad voice.

I shook my head. "You don't have to say anything. This isn't your fault, and there's nothing you can do about it."

"You, either," she replied. She turned to face me, her brown eyes deep with concern. "I don't want you to go back there, Kale."

I gave her a small smile. "That means more than you'll ever know. But I have to go back. I have to stop it. We both know that."

"But how? You've seen the gates and the guards. There's too much security to do anything."

I shrugged. It was the same question that had been circling my mind for weeks.

Her fingers traced softly along the back of my hand. She turned it over and touched the calluses that were fading on my palms. Her touch sent a tingle up my arm and I found it hard to concentrate.

"Those Galdoni had letters and numbers instead of names," she said casually as if she was thinking out loud.

"Names make us more human," I said without emotion.

She thought about it for a minute, then asked, "How'd you get your name?"

"I made it up."

She looked up at me, surprised. "You made it up?"

I nodded. "You put me on the spot. It was the first thing I could think of."

She gave a little frown. "What's your real name?"

I straightened and turned so that I leaned back against the railing and faced her, my arms folded in an effort to appear composed. I took a calming breath. "KL426."

135

Saying the name aloud forged the two worlds together. Until that moment, the Arena had seemed like a dream, and I could almost pretend it was some other life, a story from a book, something that had happened to someone else. But my heart remembered the name, and a familiar heaviness filled my limbs.

"KL426 . . . KL, Kale." Brie leaned against my arm and rested her head on my shoulder. "It doesn't matter. You are who you are, and you're a great person."

I let that sink in for a few minutes, enjoying the way it felt even though I knew it wasn't true. "Do you want to know something ironic?"

Brie looked up at my tone.

"You saw the scars on my chest from being whipped?" She nodded, her eyes tight as though she wasn't sure she wanted to hear what I was going to say. My brow furrowed. "I got a couple of them when I refused to kill AR527 when we were younger."

She stared at me for a moment, and her eyes grew bright with tears. My heart dropped and I felt terrible. "I'm sorry. I shouldn't have told you that. It's not something you should have to hear."

She shook her head. "It's not that. You deserve to tell someone. I'm not crying for me; it's that you had to go through all that. What a horrible place." She leaned against my chest and hid her face in my shirt. "I don't want you to go back. I love you."

I froze, my arms halfway up to hold her against me. My heart thundered so loud I thought the volleyball players would hear it, but they continued on oblivious of our little corner of the world, the only corner that actually felt real. "You what?" I asked softly.

Brie sniffed and looked up at me. Tears traced down her cheeks and some of her hair had escaped from her braid. "I love you," she repeated again. She gave me her special smile and I couldn't breathe.

"You. . . ." I brushed the escaped hair back behind her ear just for the excuse to touch her. I couldn't believe what she had said; my mind argued against it. "You. . . you love me?"

She nodded, her smile widening. "Is that so hard to believe?" she asked with a slightly teasing tone despite her tears.

"It is." Her smile faltered, and I rushed on. "I mean, you're not supposed to. I-I'm, well, what I am, and you're you. I mean-"

She put a finger on my lips. "Shhh. You don't make any sense when you talk like that." She stood on her tiptoes and kissed me lightly on the lips. "I love you, and I know that might take some time to get used to. But I don't want you to be hard on yourself. I think I know you better than anyone."

I shook my head. She knew a part of me, but she didn't know the monster I held inside, the one that threatened to break free and tear everything apart. If only she knew how close I had really come to killing Zach and the others. I doubted she would love me then.

"Brie, I'm not-"

She cut me off with a stern shake of her head. "Kale, you can argue all day long, but it's the heart not the head that falls in love. It might not make any sense to you, and you might not feel the same way, but that's how I feel." She paused, then dropped her eyes. A faint blush rose to her cheeks.

I realized then how much courage it had taken for her to tell me. I put a hand under her chin and tipped it up gently so that she looked at me. I found a center of calm amidst the chaos that swirled around us, and realized that the calm was from her. Her brown eyes held me, captivated me until I was no longer my own. I knew then that my heart had been hers from the beginning. "I love you." I whispered the words I never thought I would say, words a Galdoni would die for, words of weakness and at the same time of a strength so profound it filled me with awe. I could only stare at her.

"Oh, Kale," she said so quietly I barely heard her. She kissed my lips and then leaned against my chest. I wrapped my arms around her and wished we could stay there forever. I felt exhilarated, yet so afraid of the moment ending that I almost couldn't enjoy it. I knew it was wrong to fall for her, to allow her to love me, but like she said, though my head argued, my heart held all my will. I rested my chin on the top of her soft brown hair and closed my eyes.

Chapter Eleven

"Sorry to interrupt."

Brie and I both started at the sound of Jayce's voice. Brie backed up with a cute, abashed smile on her face. I studied her brother, unsure what his reaction would be.

To my surprise, he just shrugged and grinned like nothing had happened. "Hey Brie, one of the girls inside had a haircut disaster today and I told her if anyone could save it, you could."

Brie threw me another smile, the kind that crinkled her nose and laughed at being caught, and she left through the door into the house. Jayce followed her, then stopped and turned to me with his hand on the screen door.

"Just don't hurt her, that's all I ask," he said in a serious voice, his brow furrowed.

"I won't, I promise," I replied.

He nodded and disappeared into the house. I hoped deep down that I could live up to my words.

I leaned back against the porch railing. My heart pounded and my muscles ached. I wanted to fly to clear my head, but flying would only be putting the others in danger. I rubbed my eyes with one hand.

"Hey man, what's up?" Zach walked up the porch steps and took a chair near where I stood. He leaned back, propping his shoes up on the porch railing.

"Not much. Just enjoying the view." I indicated to where Rory had just face-planted in the grass in an attempt to hit a wide ball. Several other students stood around him laughing.

Zach laughed also. "Yeah, volleyball might not be the best idea. I like to observe rather than participate. Save myself for football, you know?"

I nodded and we watched in silence for a while.

There were several more bad attempts to get the ball over the sagging rope. It amazed me that the players on the other side still stuck around, but everyone seemed content to laugh at whoever's turn it was.

After a few minutes had passed, Zach put his feet back down and turned the chair so that he faced me. He cleared his throat. "It's wrong what they're doing to the Galdoni." He studied me, his expression grave.

"You know." I said it as a statement, and took a deep breath to calm the foreboding that rose in my chest.

His brow furrowed, but he nodded. "It made sense. You've been around a couple months, don't have any history or past that I can scare up, you always wear the coat, and I've never seen anyone fight like that."

"It sort of comes naturally, if you know what I mean." I gave him a tired smile.

He nodded. "I'll bet."

Silence fell as several students ran down the stairs to join the game on the back lawn. "So, what now?" I finally asked.

"You mean am I going to turn you in?" At my nod, Zach frowned. "That wouldn't be a very good way to repay you for saving my sister." Silence followed. I watched him study his hands out of the corner of my eye. He flexed one, then the other, looking at the veins on the back. He cleared his throat again. "I do have a couple questions, though."

"Shoot."

He picked at a hole in the knee of his jeans. "I don't get why they do it. Why do they fight? If it is so wrong and unethical, why don't they just say they won't kill each other?"

I pulled a chair up next to him and sat down to give myself some time to think. I tried to make sense of what I wanted to say, then finally gave up and shook my head. "It looks so black and white out here, away from the Academy.

But when you're there, fighting and trying to survive is all you know." A memory swept through me.

Two older Galdoni were beating on a younger one who had been punished for stealing food and was being starved. He had snuck out of the barracks one night and broken the kitchen lock. Guards found him and we had all been called out in the middle of the night to participate in his punishment. When volunteers were called for, about half the group raised their hands. The young Galdoni looked so scared I couldn't bring myself to join them.

Two were chosen and told to beat him until the whistle was blown. The young Galdoni tried to fight back, but by the time they were finished, he would feel his punishment for a long time.

"Now, what did he do wrong?" the lead guard in lean black armor asked. He tossed a serrated knife in the air and caught it by the blade, then did it again, catching it by the handle.

"He stole food," one of the younger Galdoni said in a tentative voice.

"Wrong!" the lead guard yelled. His voice echoed down the hall like the crack of a whip. He backhanded the Galdoni who had spoken. "That's for giving the wrong answer." He then kicked the boy in the gut and he fell to the ground gasping. "And that's for saying it like a coward!"

He turned and glared at the rest of us. "What did PK309 do wrong?"

"He didn't fight!" an older Galdoni yelled out.

The guard sneered down at the beaten Galdoni. "He tried, but he didn't fight." He raised his voice. "Is trying fighting?"

141

"If you try, you die," we shouted together one of the mantras that had been drilled into us until it pounded with our heartbeats.

"You must do," the lead guard said. "Those who fail to do, die." He glared at the two Galdoni who had carried out the beating. "Take him away."

I shook my head and pulled myself back to the present. "It's kill or be killed in there. When that's all that matters, it truly becomes *all* that matters. And you're taught to believe that your life is only worth those whom you can kill."

"But don't they know it's wrong?" Zach gave me a frank stare. "You know it's wrong."

I met his gaze. "I know it's wrong because I've lived outside of it. If I had met you in the Arena, there'd be four fewer humans in the world."

His face paled slightly, but he didn't look away. "I don't believe you."

An example came to mind from my history class. I opened a hand. "Take terrorist attacks. People have been raised to believe that this nation is full of corrupt, satanic people whose mere presence defiles the world. They believe that they are following the wishes of their maker by destroying even just a few, and usually at the cost of their own lives. And why do they do it? Because that's the way they've been raised. It's all they know, all they've been taught to believe, and they have no reason to question those beliefs."

"So the answer is to give them a reason to question?"

I nodded with a slight frown. "Yes, but the real problem is how to do it. Do you think if the nation says, look, we aren't bad people, anyone will listen?"

He shook his head.

I agreed. "No, of course not. And therein lies the conundrum."

He put his feet against the railing and pushed back so that his chair balanced on two legs. "There's got to be a way."

I glanced at him. "To end terrorism or to stop the Galdoni from killing each other?"

"Both." He smiled. "And maybe to keep us from killing the Galdoni."

I fought back a smile. "That would be good."

We sat in amiable silence for a few minutes, then he asked, "What about the masks?"

"What do you mean?"

Zach's brow furrowed. "Is there something special about them or are they just part of the armor? I've never seen a Galdoni battle where they don't wear them."

My gut tightened and I ran my fingers along the wooden railing beside me. "The masks are sacred," I said quietly.

Zach nodded as if he had expected something like that. "How so?"

My breathing slowed as I thought of the lectures and of the rituals that were pounded into us until we accepted them without question, and believed them without suspicion. I took a deep breath. "The Arena sands are sacred, our trying ground for heaven. The masks show our respect for the Arena."

"What would happen if you fought without one?"

I shook my head and rubbed my brow. "No Galdoni would enter the Arena without a mask or take his mask off during battle. To do so would forfeit one's chance of making it into heaven."

"Do you believe that?" Zach asked quietly without any hint of derision or judgment in his voice.

"I don't know what I believe anymore," I admitted. "My whole world has turned upside down."

143

Zach gave me a sympathetic glance and let the topic go. I watched the volleyball players, but my mind stayed in the Arena.

***

We got home well past midnight, but none of us felt quite ready for bed. Brie and Jayce checked in with their dad, then came over to lounge on the sofas and chat about insignificant things while Nikko clicked away on his laptop searching for information for yet another of his research projects. Brie rested her head on my shoulder and Jayce sprawled on the other couch with one foot on the top cushion and the other on the floor.

Jayce and I talked about other animal traits Galdoni could have used. We had gone through the major defense abilities of the common predators and Jayce was now reaching for any we had missed. It took several minutes for my mind to register that I could no longer hear the rhythmic click of Nikko's typing.

"How about long necks like a giraffe?"

"Why, so we could eat from tall trees or something?" I replied with a glance at Nikko. His brow was furrowed and lips tight as he stared at the computer screen.

Jayce laughed and slapped his knee.

Nikko's jaw twitched from gritting his teeth.

"What's up, Nikko?" I asked, concerned.

"Or a beaver's tail," Jayce continued, oblivious. "Could be handy if you ever want to take up pottery."

Brie noticed Nikko's lack of response and sat up. "Nik, whatcha looking at?"

Nikko finally looked up. He met my gaze. "It's not pleasant."

At Nikko's tone, Jayce stopped laughing at his own jokes and sat up straight.

Nikko turned the computer so we could see the headlines.

145

"Galdoni Attack Citizens in Bar, One Dead, Three Injured," a news page proclaimed.

My heart skipped a beat. "There must be a mistake. They wouldn't attack defenseless civilians, would they?"

Nikko rubbed his eyes. "It says they were in the back corner of a bar at a table when the Arena fight aired. No one noticed them because they wore long coats." He glanced at me but continued, "Apparently, some guys in the bar started joking about the fight and saying derogatory things about Galdoni, and the two Galdoni attacked. By the time the police got there, the place was torn apart."

"And the Galdoni?" Jayce asked.

"One was shot, and the other taken back to the Academy."

Silence filled the room. It pressed around me until I couldn't breathe. I rubbed my palms on my knees in an effort to bring the feeling back to my hands. "That's really bad. How is anyone going to accept Galdoni into normal society with this kind of stuff happening?"

Nikko stared at me. "You have a plan?"

I shook my head. "No, just something Zach and I were talking about."

Brie stared at me and Nikko's eyes widened. "You mean, he knows?"

At my nod, Jayce hurried to the window and peered out into the night. "Are you crazy?" he said over his shoulder. "He probably told the cops."

"No. We have an understanding." Jayce looked at me like I was crazy and I shrugged. "He called it a fair trade for me saving his sister. I trust him."

Jayce glanced out the window one more time and shook his head. "Okay; it's your decision." He sat back down on the couch and gestured at the computer. "But that's definitely not going to help things."

"Not at all." I rose and made my way to the bedroom. "I'm going to try to get some shut-eye. See you guys in the morning."

I closed the door behind me and settled on the bed, but too much had happened for sleep to claim my weary brain. I felt caged, trapped, like the inevitable was drawing closer and I wouldn't have my freedom much longer. Finally, I couldn't take it anymore. I opened the door, made my way through the now empty living room, and left through the back door into the welcoming embrace of night.

I walked through the trees behind the house, grateful for the darkness of a new moon. I had left my coat at the house, a careless move, but I doubted anyone was out and it was too dark to see clearly anyway. I found a clearing and took to the sky.

The wind filled my wings as though the sky had missed me as much as I had missed flying. It felt so good to feel the air through my feathers. I beat down hard until I flew so high the cold breeze ran a chill down my spine. Lights dotted the houses below, warm windows where families slept unshaken by the hypocrisy of their callous world.

The judgment was harsh because I was entangled in the human world more than a Galdoni was supposed to be. I wanted to be a part of it so badly, but I kept seeing AR527's face, still and cold as the high night sky. As good as it felt to fly, I couldn't chase away the foreboding in the back of my mind. I knew I had to make it stop somehow.

I pushed away all thought and flew as hard and as fast as I could. The wind rushed past my face, stealing my breath as the crispness brought tears to my eyes. My wings ached to fly faster and I obeyed. I dove and rose with the swells, circled buildings and followed winding roads until I flew above checkered farms and sleepy cattle. The scent of fresh-cut hay tickled my nose.

I flew low enough to run my fingers along sheaths of wheat, soft and ready for harvest. I followed the ditch that watered the fields to the river that fed it. A few ducks and drowsy killdeer started at my appearance, but I was gone before they could make a sound. A beat of my wings brought me above a quiet town of scattered houses and a lone church. I circled the church once, questions crowding my head. I shoved them deep inside and flew away into the night.

I kept telling myself that Brie, Jayce, and Nikko would be better off if I didn't return, that my presence brought them danger and I didn't want to hurt them. But Brie's voice was constantly in the back of my mind, her words a whisper above my dark thoughts. I heard her say 'I love you' so many times I almost let myself believe that it was okay, that I wasn't a monster, that loving me wouldn't turn her into a monster, too. I almost believed it.

Regardless of my intentions, I recognized the buildings as the wind brought me back. I barely glided, my wings heavy with the unaccustomed strain. They ached when I finally landed in the small forest, but it was a good ache and my body relished the feeling. I felt more alive than I ever had before, and more torn by my two battling lives. It seemed that everything in my life was a battle somehow.

All thoughts fell away when I stepped through the trees and saw Brie asleep on Nikko's back porch, a blanket slid halfway off her shoulders and a flashlight lying dim with low batteries next to her foot. Starlight played across her face like tiny fairies soothing her with their soft songs of midnight. Her hair, pulled from its braid, fell across her cheek, the brown strands turned to gold by the faint light that spilled through the window behind her.

At that moment, I didn't want to go back to the Academy so badly my chest ached.

I walked quietly up the steps and eased down next to her. I opened my wings, grateful for the cover of night, and pulled her close. Brie leaned on my shoulder for a few minutes and I listened to her breathing change as she awoke. It reminded me of when I first met her and a smile touched my face.

"Kale?" Her voice was quiet, disbelieving. She turned her face to look up at me and I saw the tear tracks on her cheeks. "Kale? I came here to talk to you and you were gone. I was afraid you wouldn't come back."

My heart constricted and I held my breath, afraid of the feelings my heart already gave away. "I had to come back," I finally forced myself to say.

The tears in her eyes caught the starlight. "Because of me?"

I shook my head. "Because I have a test tomorrow." Her brow furrowed and I smiled. "Of course, because of you." She laughed and slapped my shoulder; I pulled her close. She rested her head on my chest and I imagined that she could hear the way my heart skipped a beat just from being so close to her. "Brie, I-I don't want to hurt you."

"Then say you'll stay."

"You know I can't do that," I replied quietly, even though I wanted to say the words she asked to hear so intensely they almost came out instead.

"I know," she said after a few moments, her voice muffled against my shirt.

I drew my wings in closer around us. "Brie." She looked up at the sound of my voice. I forced the truth past my trembling heart. "Brie, I love you. I love you so much it

149

scares me." Saying the words made a fear I had never experienced before grab ahold of my heart like a clawed demon; it was the fear of losing something I loved.

Brie must have seen it in my face, because she held me tight as though she would never let me go. "I love you, too. Just promise me that if we can find a way to stop it, you won't go back to the Academy."

I rested my chin on the top of her head. Her scent filled my senses. I took a deep breath and let it out slowly. "I promise," I breathed into her hair. She held me tighter and I closed my wings around us.

The silence, so perfect that I barely dared to breathe for fear of breaking the spell that held us together, finally drifted away when Brie sat up. She leaned against me, her brow furrowed. "Tell me something about when you were younger."

"There aren't many pleasant memories," I replied carefully.

"Tell me anything. I feel like you had to go through it all by yourself. I want to know what you went through."

I searched my mind for something that wasn't too dark or violent. One memory came to the forefront and I hesitated. "Well, there is one."

She nodded encouragingly. "Go on."

I closed my eyes and saw the papers piled untidily on a desk. They were covered front to back in a hurried, tight penmanship, lines scratched out and tiny sketches drawn where words failed.

"Roommates were rotated on a weekly basis so that we didn't become more than acquaintances with any other Galdoni. But one particular roommate, SR587, and I, somehow skipped the rotation and stayed together for a couple of weeks." I could see him sitting hunched in the corner of his pallet with a pad of paper on one knee as he squinted in the faint light.

"I'd never met anyone like him. He didn't talk much, which was fine because I didn't either. But he continuously paced around our tiny room like he was going to explode. Then he would rush to the bed, grab his pen, and write like mad until the next training session. Of course, he always hid everything under his mattress in case the guard showed up for a room check."

"What did he write?"

"Poetry."

"Poetry!" The surprise on Brie's face reflected how I had felt the first time I took a chance and read one of SR's poems.

"He started to confide in me," I remembered. "He said that the poetry filled his thoughts to the point that if he didn't write it down, he couldn't think anymore. He had a book of poems one of the teachers had snuck him and he hid it like it was gold."

The well-leafed pages were soft with use, the lines faded with the number of times he had run his fingers over them in the faint light. I could see the dog-eared corners and creased leather binding, its worn gold title and acknowledgment of authors barely discernible on the cover and spine.

"What happened to him?" she asked quietly.

"One day I came back to find the room in shambles. The bed was overturned and pages were everywhere. I never saw him again." I toyed with a string that hung from the sleeve of my shirt. "It felt wrong to leave the pages like that, so I picked them up and sat them on the desk. I stared at them for the longest time, sure someone would come and take them away. But it felt wrong that they would be destroyed and no one would know what he wrote."

"So you read them?"

I nodded. "I memorized as many as I could. The guards came sooner than I expected and I sat on my bed and pretended like I couldn't have cared less when they put the pages in a garbage can and burned them in the middle of the Arena for all the Galdoni to see." The memory brought back a faint whiff of burning paper and dreams.

She looked up at me. "Do you remember any of them."

I nodded. I quietly recited my favorite one.

"In its haunted hollow my heart screams softly,
Give me voice and I will tear this world;
But I dare not because the world is already torn.
In a fit of silence my hands plead,
Give me a weapon and I will be break you free;
But I dare not because the world is not my home.
In the prison cell my wings call my name,
Open me and I will give you flight;
But I would not because I have no dreams.
In its quiet slumber my spirit whispers,
Hear my words and I will give you peace;
But I could not because I have no soul.
In the Arena grand the sword beckons me,
Your life is mine and I will take what you owe;
But I prevail, because as nothing I cannot die."

Brie sat in silence for a few minutes. "How old were you when he was taken away?" she asked softly.

"Not sure. We didn't really keep track of our ages at the Academy, but it was before my first kill."

She shook her head and leaned back against me. A slight breeze stirred her hair and I raised my wings to shield us from the night.

She tucked her head under my chin and I felt her breathing slow as she fell to sleep. I was about to nod off as well when she whispered, "You promised."

"I know," I replied softly.

Chapter Twelve

I found Nikko the next day at the kitchen table before sunup. "What are you doing?"

He glanced at me sheepishly. "Looking for a way out." He turned the computer and I saw the Arena from one of the inside cameras. It looked forlorn and empty in the low light.

"Whoa. How'd you get that?"

"I breached their security site; a couple tricks I picked up from a friend."

I watched as he switched from one camera to the next. It took us in an entire three hundred and sixty degree view of the Arena. "Guess they didn't want to miss a good shot."

"Guess not." He ran a hand through his hair and blew out a breath. "The problem is, I can't find a way out. I've studied every view and that place is tight."

I glanced at him and saw the circles under his eyes. "How long have you been doing this?"

He gave a tired smile. "Since yesterday."

I stared at him in surprise. "Through the night?"

He nodded as he tabbed through the screens again, faster this time. "But there's no point. Everywhere I look there're bars, electrified walls, laser security- it's tighter than the White House."

"Afraid to let their lab pets get back into society."

He turned to see if I was joking, and gave a weary laugh when he saw I was. But his smile quickly vanished. "Kale, I don't see a way out. We have to stop this before you get back there."

"We'll find a way," I reassured him, touched by the urgency in his voice. "There's got to be a way." I turned back to the screen before he could see the doubt on my face.

CHEREE ALSOP

"Kale?" He waited until I looked at him. "It's wrong, you know?"

I nodded, but his brows drew together in frustration.

"No, I mean, it's really wrong. My father's a doctor, and he's taken an oath to do no harm. Yet here are other doctors of medicine creating life in order for it to be destroyed for entertainment?" He shook his head. "If that's not an example of doing harm, I don't know what is." He rubbed his eyes in agitation.

I put a hand on his shoulder. "Nikko, you're not responsible for this, and neither is ninety-nine percent of the rest of the world. You didn't create it, and the people who actually watch this stuff probably don't stop to think about what's really happening." At least, I hoped that was the case.

Nikko shook his head. "They know deep down that it's wrong. They must. I hope that they have a conscience that tells them watching somebody die for their entertainment is wrong; otherwise, I've completely lost faith in humanity."

I gave a small smile. "You know, when I first learned from Brie that the Arena battles were aired for gambling, it destroyed my vision of what life was like outside the Arena." I gestured at Nikko's house. "But being here and living a real life of my own with friends and," I hesitated, then said, "Love. It's like nothing I could ever have imagined."

Nikko smiled and put a hand on my shoulder. "It's good to have you here. There's got to be a way so you don't have to go back to the Academy."

I shrugged. "Regardless of what happens, this has been worth a lifetime behind those walls."

Nikko turned back to the computer, his brow creased with determination. "I'd rather give you a lifetime in front of them instead."

After school, Jayce joined us with his own computer. Nikko helped him hack into the Academy security system, and he was able to single out cameras in the individual cells.

We watched a Galdoni about fifteen years old be thrown into a cell. His face was bruised and he limped over to the pallet on the floor that served as a bed. He sat in the corner with his arms around his knees and stared at the opposite wall, a blank expression on his battered face.

I couldn't tear my eyes away. The pallet, the gray scratched, windowless walls, barred door, low ceiling, and a floor covered in filth that would never wash away no matter how hard we were pushed to scrub it. The solitary room, reserved for Galdoni who acted out, had been my home many nights. The regular quarters weren't much better, but at least they had windows, even though they were barred and tiny. It was amazing how much the light of day could lift the heart.

The expressionless stare on the Galdoni's face tore at my soul. My own face remembered it with an ache, the wall that kept all emotion in, that felt no pain, and that hid the only thing the guards could never take away. No matter how they tried to break us, I never let go of what it was that made me myself. No matter how many Galdoni let go of themselves and became mindless beasts, whatever essence that spoke through my bones would always be my own.

"How do they keep people like that?" Disgust filled Jayce's voice.

"Not people," I reminded him quietly. He opened his mouth to argue and I shook my head. "It's how they justify it. It took me a long time to realize that by treating us like animals, they could believe that's what we were. It's the only way I think they could sleep at night. The few teachers that acted out for us were never seen again, so the rest learned to rebel quietly by giving us books and things we could keep hidden. They taught us about the real world outside the Academy walls, hoping that one day we could see it."

"It's not right," Jayce growled. "How are we supposed to have faith in a justice system when *people*," he stressed the word in a tone that gave no room for argument, "Are treated like this without just cause?"

I fought back a smile and he glared at me. "What?"

I couldn't help the grin that came to my face. "I might have deserved it once in a while."

Nikko sat back in his chair, his brows pulled together. "What did you do?"

I shrugged. "I might have set a couple of fires on more than a few occasions." I laughed at their stares. "The Academy still has to obey fire marshal law. Whenever the fire alarms go off, all Galdoni are forced to evacuate to the Arena. It gave us a chance to stretch our wings." I chuckled, remembering, "It got to the point that whenever the alarm went off, they came immediately to my room to see what was burning." I rubbed a hand on my chest at the remembered pain.

Brie came in with a plate of ham, cheese, and egg sandwiches, interrupting our conversation. Allie followed close behind her. Nikko and Jayce shut their laptops before they could see what we were watching. Brie eyed them both suspiciously, then shook her head. "I don't know what you boys are up to, but you need a break." She took a closer look at Nikko. "And some sleep. I don't know how you plan to stop anything if your brains can't even function properly."

"So you admit that I have one," Jayce pointed out with a grin.

She swatted at him and he jumped out of the way. "I never said how big it was."

"Bigger than yours," he replied.

"Oh, yeah?" She grabbed a pillow off the couch and threw it at him. He ducked and it hit her books off the chair, spilling all her papers onto the ground. "Hey!"

"You threw it!" he argued. Allie giggled and hid behind me.

I bent to help pick up the papers when a knock sounded at the door. We all froze and looked at each other. My coat was in the bedroom. I had gotten way too comfortable without it.

I rushed to my room and threw on the coat before Jayce opened the door. To my surprise, I came back out to find Zach standing there with another student I had seen a couple of times around school.

Zach glanced around quickly and his face lit up when he saw me. "Kale," he said, pushing past Nikko. "I figured it out!"

I glanced at the black bag he carried. "Figured what out?"

Jayce shoved the door shut behind him with a grumble as Zach tossed the bag onto the table. "The truth problem. You said that the way to stop this is to give the people a reason to question what was happening, right?"

I nodded. "Yeah, so?"

"So we give them the truth. You know, a 'Ye shall know the truth, and the truth shall make you free' sort of thing."

"Why is the jock quoting the Bible?" Jayce mumbled to Brie. She shrugged, her brow furrowed.

"I'm surprised you know the Bible," Nikko whispered back to him. Jayce elbowed him in the ribs.

Zach ignored them. "Kale, this is Iggy, short for Iguana, which is short for whatever other foreign name he has."

The other student looked me up and down with a frank expression. "So you're the Galdoni, huh?" He said it as more

158

of a statement than a question, and a not-very-impressed statement at that.

I saw Jayce bristle and held up a hand. "Yes, and you're here why?"

"He's the tech guru." Zach explained offhandedly. "He'll be the one making the movie."

"Movie?" Brie asked.

Zach gave her an impatient look and said in carefully spaced words, "We're making a movie about the Galdoni so that people won't fear them. That way, they'll see Galdoni as human and not as animals." A slight frown crossed his face. "The only problem will be getting video from the Academy."

"That's no problem," Nikko said. He spun one of the laptops around and opened it.

Zach and Iggy stared at the form of the young Galdoni in the tiny room. I heard Brie's intake of breath and realized we hadn't prepared her. I gave her a small smile and she dropped her eyes, her lips tight.

"Awesome!" Zach said.

"Let's get started," Iggy echoed.

***

After hours of running through images from the monitors and the storage databases Nikko managed to hack, I finally had to leave. None of them stopped me when I slipped out the back door and shut it behind me. The closed door felt like a barrier between me and the images on the screens. I took a deep breath of the rain-tinged air and fought the urge to fly.

Instead, I stepped down the stairs from the porch and let the rain fall on my head and shoulders. I lifted my face to the starless night sky and let the cold drops chase the thoughts from my head. I wanted to throw off the coat and stretch my wings, but I fought back the impulse.

A few minutes later, the door opened behind me and I heard the creak of footsteps down the stairs. "You'll catch a cold getting soaked like that."

I smiled at Brie's worried expression. "I like it. We never got to feel the rain at the Academy, but it was always one of my favorite sounds."

She nestled under my arm and we stood quietly for a few minutes listening to the sound of the rain falling around us. For that single moment, it felt like we were the only two people left on earth, like the chaos of the world had disappeared with the rumble of thunder through the trees.

Brie took a breath. "I love the smell of rain. It's how I imagine heaven will be like."

I gave her a small smile.

"What?" she asked quietly.

I shook my head. "I don't want to ruin this."

A little frown touched her lips. "You don't believe in heaven?"

I gave her a half smile. "Oh, I believe in heaven." I turned my face away so she couldn't see my expression. "But the views of heaven are a little messed-up at the Academy and I'm starting to doubt what I used to believe. You have to have a soul to get there."

Brie stiffened under my arm. "You have a soul."

I frowned slightly and avoided meeting her gaze. "Where do souls come from?"

"From God," she said without hesitation.

"Where do Galdoni come from?"

"From God," she said again, but her voice was less certain.

I shook my head with a sad smile and looked at her. "Galdoni were created by men playing God."

She gave a defiant shrug. "You wouldn't be alive if you didn't have a soul. A soul is what makes you who you are."

"I believe I have a soul as much as a bird or a dog has a soul, but I'm not sure if there's a place in heaven for them, either."

She frowned. "Sure there is."

"You're a dreamer."

"I'm a realist," she replied.

"A realist dreamer."

She shook her head with a laugh, the somber mood broken. "There's no such thing!"

"There is now. You'll have a heaven all to yourself; of course, you'll have to share it with all the dogs and birds."

She leaned against my chest. "It wouldn't be heaven without you."

I took in the scent of her lavender hair shampoo and the slight hint of floral perfume that defied the masking rain; my heart contracted. "I'm already in heaven."

161

She hugged me tight and I wrapped my arms around her. We didn't let go of each other until Jayce opened the back door and hollered for us to come see their rough draft.

Chapter Thirteen

Iggy clicked a button and then turned the laptop so we could watch. My heart slowed at the first picture. A pair of white-gloved hands held a newborn baby so small that with its feet tucked up it fit comfortably in the groove the cupped hands made. Beside the sweet, innocent, peaceful expression on the sleeping baby's face, the thing that stood out most was the pair of delicate white wings folded about its shoulders. Brie's breath caught and she leaned against me. I put an arm around her.

The next slide showed a toddler with his hands out as he took what appeared to be his first steps. Beautiful tan wings, the color of a mourning dove's breast, were held open as he used them for balance. His face practically glowed with excitement and he looked normal and happy, but it was hard to ignore the lab equipment around him, the stainless steel tables, microscopes, and rolling chairs that would be a hazard for any baby so young. On one chubby wrist he wore a red armband, the kind used in hospitals to keep mothers and babies together. I could remember the feel of that band, and the first time I read the numbers and letters that became my name.

The next slide showed a room full of toddlers, each with beautiful wings so soft and downy and arms and legs so chunky and full it looked like a room of cherubs. The toddlers were sitting in rows on a gray carpet, and one had a smile on his innocent face.

In the next slide, a guard leaned across to the smiling toddler with a whip bearing down. Even though Iggy didn't show the follow-up image, it was easy to read by the fear on the face of the toddler and the other children around him

163

what was about to happen. I closed my eyes briefly but didn't turn away.

The next slide showed a classroom of winged children sitting by age group, heads bent as they worked. The scene seemed innocent enough until one noticed the ankle bands and cords that secured them to each desk.

Brie gasped at the next image and turned her head into my shoulder. A young boy about six years old stood in the middle of a fighting circle. A katana dangled from his fingers, its tip resting on the ground. Dark blood ran slowly down the blade to the floor. The boy's head hung low, and his wings, the tawny shade of a lion's mane, drooped in dejected sorrow. At the boy's feet lay another boy, his eyes closed tight against the pain of the life-stealing wound across his stomach. Blood pooled around them both, reflecting darkly off the bright arena walls.

Iggy had zoomed in on the same picture in the next image, showing only the bowed face of the boy with the blade. A tear slid slowly down his cheek, his eyes shut tight as though to block out what he had done.

The next slide showed two teenage boys in brutal combat. One held a wickedly spiked mace sideways above him and slid across the arena floor on his knees while the other leaped into the air, dark wings open and his back arched as he brought a sword down toward his opponent.

I stared at him. Time stood still as I remembered the weight of the sword in my hands, its pommel cold and smooth in my grasp. "That's me," I said quietly.

"What?" Brie asked, but Nikko and Iggy nodded their heads.

I pointed needlessly to the boy in the air, poised for a deadly strike. "I remember that fight."

Brie touched the screen; her fingers lightly grazed the bleeding gash down the forearm of the black-haired boy. She glanced back at me and her gaze lingered on the matching scar. She shook her head and I saw tears in her eyes. She turned without a word and left the room.

"Brie," I called after her.

Jayce touched my shoulder. "Let her go. She's dealing with some hard stuff."

I stared after her, my chest tight. "Yeah, because of me."

Jayce's grip tightened and he turned me to face him. "Because you're worth it," he said; his tone gave no room for argument. "All of this is worth it if it keeps you out of the Arena and out of *that* again." He pointed at the screen.

I didn't have a reply.

"The way I see it," Iggy spoke as though nothing had happened. "The best way to catch the biggest audience is to show this during the Blood Match."

The others nodded and though it was still a few weeks away, I had to agree. All the statistics showed that viewers nearly tripled during the biggest fight of the season where the best fighters from earlier months fought to the death. It was what we as Galdoni prepared for our whole lives, and what I had found out many viewers saved a year's wages to gamble on.

"Can it be ready by then?" I asked, trying to push the images I had found on the internet of the last couple of Death Matches from my mind.

"Definitely," Iggy replied. "Add more slides, some heart-wrenching music, and a gripping note at the end, and I think even Vegas would have to agree that this is wrong."

***

"I don't know if this is such a good idea," I said, watching a group of kids run by at breakneck speed with a small football.

"Sure it is," Jayce replied with a grin. "The Doc said you needed to experience student life, and what's more student life than a football game?" He handed a couple of dollars and our student cards to the bored young man at the ticket booth who handed back the cards and four tickets.

"Besides," Nikko said from my other side. "Zach invited you and it would be rude not to show up."

"I just feel like we're pushing it." We were jostled through the gates and I stared up uneasily at the crowd filling the stands on either side of the aisle.

Brie took my arm reassuringly and we walked together up the shallow steps to the top. "It'll be fine. You might even have fun," she said with a teasing smile.

I settled beside her on the hard metal bench and watched the red and yellow team run through stretches and cardio exercises. Across the fence on the practice field, the other team in black and green tossed a football and performed several drills.

"And you get to watch the cheerleaders," Jayce said, nudging me with his elbow. "Especially Kara and Katelyn." He gestured to two blondes at the end of the cheerleading row shouting warm up cheers to the crowd. Several boys on the front bench yelled the cheers back at the top of their lungs.

"Looks like you have competition," I said.

"No one is competition," Jayce replied, leaning back on the bench with a dramatic sigh.

Brie just rolled her eyes. "Boys."

I glanced down the aisle and saw Dane making his way through the crowd with his two minions close behind. He was a few seats away when he looked up and met my gaze. His eyes widened and he stumbled back into his companions. They looked from him to me and they both tensed; all three then turned and disappeared into the crowd. I focused on the field, but kept a look out in case they returned.

A whistle blew and the game began. It took me a while to forget about Dane and keep my attention on the game, but the defensive and offensive tactics appealed to my battle sense. It was interesting to see the way Zach avoided the rushers and threw the football without getting hit. His defensive line was shorter than the other team, but they made up for it with aggression.

"You'd make a good football player," Nikko observed, his feet propped on the bench in front of us.

I laughed. "I don't know if the pads would fit."

Jayce leaned forward. "Imagine what kind of a game it would be if they could fly!"

A lady in front of us with long black hair piled on her head and strict black glasses glanced back disapprovingly. Jayce sat up and turned his attention back to the game.

I had learned about football from several professors at the Academy who were obvious enthusiasts, but it was different actually watching the game in person, feeling the rush when a running back carried the ball past the defenders, hearing the roar of the crowd when a team scored a touchdown. I thoroughly enjoyed the ballpark hot dogs Nikko bought, and Brie shared her purple cotton candy with everyone. I even got caught up yelling some of the cheers back at the cheerleaders with Jayce.

I began to see similarities between football and the Arena battles. Each side had supporters and people who wanted to

167

see the other team fail; I even saw money exchange hands on more than one occasion. Each side fought for honor, and gave their all no matter how hard the going got.

Then Zach went down after a hard hit and it took him several minutes to rise. I stood up along with the rest of the audience and waited while his medical team attended to him. I wondered if the crowd for the other team hoped he would stay down, but when Zach rose back to his feet and waved at the audience to let them know he was alright, a roar of relief went up from both sides of the small school stadium.

I looked at the people around me, wondering how they could be so relieved that Zach wasn't injured, but could watch a television show where the entire goal was for one of the contestants to die. It was hard to push the thought aside and enjoy the rest of the game.

Our team won by a close margin that had everyone standing on their feet and yelling by the time the game was over. The Warriors ran off the field triumphant, shaking hands with the Cobras in a show of sportsmanship I found amazing considering the fact that they had lost. I wondered briefly how it would be if the Arena battles ended without bloodshed and the winner shook hands with the loser, each leaving the dome with their lives and dignity still intact.

Brie saw some of her friends across the field and left to talk with them for a minute. Jayce and Nikko made their way to the cheerleaders; I leaned against the fence by the field and watched their fumbling attempts to strike up a conversation.

"What'd you think?" Zach asked.

I turned to find him in sweatpants and a Warriors tee-shirt. "It was amazing," I said honestly. "You were great."

"I have a good team," Zach replied. He tossed me the football he was carrying. "Here, let's play."

I shook my head and tried to give it back. "I'd better not. You're probably worn out from the game and I don't want to draw any attention."

"Hey," he said with a grin. "If I was worn out, I wouldn't have given you a football. Give it a try."

He held open his hands and I threw it underhand into them.

"Come on, now," he said with a challenging grin. "Give me your best." He stepped back a few yards and threw me a tight spiral.

I caught it against my chest and he jogged back over to me. "Catch it like this," he said, holding his hands out with his fingers close together but not touching to create a buffer for the ball. He tossed it up in the air and caught it on the way back down to demonstrate, then he backed up and threw it again.

I caught it the way he had shown me, then chucked it awkwardly back at him.

He shook his head and returned to my side. "Hold it with your fingers between the laces toward the end of the ball, like this." He showed me his grip, then put my hand on the ball the same way. "The laces keep your grip firm and if you flick your wrist as you let go, it'll give it the tight spin."

He backed up again and I threw it softly. It spun in a slow spiral and he grinned when he caught it. "Perfect, now put some zip into it!" He jogged further down the field, then threw it at his full speed; it stung my hands when I caught it.

I threw it back faster this time and the ball barely wobbled in its spiral. He threw it back and yelled, "I know you're stronger than that. Show me something!"

I took a breath and stepped into the throw, putting my full strength behind it. The ball zipped toward Zach like a dart to a dartboard, and his eyes widened as he reached out to

169

catch it. The ball hit his hands, and the force of it drove it back to his chest. His breath left him in an audible whoosh and he staggered back a few steps. He stared at the ball for a second before jogging slowly back to me. I glanced over and saw several younger kids watching me with wide eyes and open mouths. I walked to meet Zach.

He handed me the ball, then rubbed his hands together. "Geesh, man. That was a rocket!" He looked me up and down. "I need to get you on the team. Of course, Coach would probably replace me with you, but dang!"

I shook my head with a grin. "I don't think the uniform would fit. Besides, we've gotta give the other team at least a chance."

Zach laughed so hard he had to double over with his hands on his knees to catch his breath.

***

The next morning someone had written a word I didn't recognize in black marker on the front of my locker. I grabbed my Biology book out, then shut it to show Jayce who was standing nearby. "What does this mean?"

His eyebrows lifted slightly, but he shrugged. "It's just another way to say hello."

I looked at it again skeptically. "Are you sure?"

"Sure I'm sure. Someone's just being friendly." He glanced back at the locker again, then threw his arm over my shoulder and steered me to class. "Brie's waiting. We don't want to make her upset by being late."

I entered the classroom and nodded at Dr. Ray as we passed his desk on the way to our seats. "Hello, Dr. Ray," I said, but I used the word from my locker in the place of hello in an effort to expand my vocabulary.

Dr. Ray stared at me, his eyebrows lifted. He then tapped a pencil eraser on his desk and glanced at Jayce. "Is this your work?"

Jayce shrugged, his cheeks red, and hurried to his seat.

A smile touched the corners of Dr. Ray's lips. "Kale, there are some words we don't use at this school. That happened to be one of them." He threw a look at Jayce. "Next time, if Jayce tells you to say something, don't."

I nodded, fighting back a smile as well, and went to my desk. On my way past Jayce, I smacked him on the back of the head. "Hey!" he said.

"You mean *hello*?" I asked, leaning down to say the word quiet enough that Dr. Ray wouldn't overhear.

Jayce's mouth fell open and he stared at me, then he started to laugh. He rubbed the back of his head. "Yeah, I mean hello."

"Jayce!" Dr. Ray growled from across the room.
"Sorry," Jayce said, ducking his head to hide a laugh.
I chuckled and took my seat.

***

I fell back from the others when we walked to school the next morning. Red and gold leaves drifted slowly from the trees and twirled in a breeze that smelled of rich earth and the promise of cold. The air carried a crisp bite to it that I had never felt before, and I held each breath in my lungs as long as I could.

The early morning sky was pale blue with a blush of pink between the trees as the last of the sunrise faded. It was such a contrast from cold cement walls, metal bars, and stone-faced guards that I wanted to stop and watch the progress of night into day in order to catch each nuance of a world I had never known. It felt like every second the day changed to something new and completely different from the moment before.

A bird sang above us; I was searching for him between the thinning leaves when a shoulder jostled me back to the present. "What I'd tell you! Three numbers. Read them. Three!"

I stared at Jayce. "What are you talking about?"

"Did you call them?" Nikko challenged. "Probably some mental institution or a school for the emotionally dwarfed."

Jayce glowered at him. "For your information, all three told me they would answer anytime I called."

"Who are you talking about?" I asked.

"Cheerleaders!" Jayce said triumphantly. "I got three of the cheerleaders' phone numbers!"

I threw Brie a questioning glance and she just shrugged in exasperation. "Men."

"Not all men stoop to the-" Nikko was interrupted by several students running by.

"Angela, what's going on?" Jayce shouted.

One of the girls turned, her face pale. "John's on the roof of the old city building. He's going to jump!" She hurried to catch up to her friends.

We exchanged glances, then ran after them.

A big crowd had formed around the old building a block from the high school. The structure towered above anything surrounding it, but the architecture was old and clusters of bricks were missing from the walls. The building had been locked up after the new city building was built three years ago; it was scheduled to be demolished, but the demolition date kept getting put off. The locks were often picked and one of my duties on my nightly rounds was to make sure no one was in the building.

The people that surrounded the usually ignored structure stared up at a form on the roof. He waved and shouted for them to move away, but several of the onlookers bravely stood where he would hit if he jumped.

I found Mr. Mason, the head of security and my boss, near the front. "Who's taking care of this?"

"The cops handle jumper situations. We aren't allowed to get involved. I called them already but they sure are taking their sweet time." His brow creased worriedly and he looked back up at the roof, shading his eyes against the morning sun.

I wasn't sure what the cops normally did in that type of situation, but I knew time was essential and they were definitely running out of it. The student on the roof moved and everyone gasped.

"His dad committed suicide last year, shot himself in the head in front of his entire family," a girl next to me said to her friend. "He's really struggled since."

"He's in my biology class," a boy with spacers in his ears replied. "He's quiet, but I never thought he'd do something like this."

174

Brie touched my arm. "This is horrible."

"We've got to do something," I replied.

"Yes, but what-"

I was already making my way to the edge of the crowd. She followed me around the building to the back door. I pulled out my keys.

"You're going in?"

I answered her question by unlocking the door.

We ran across the hall to the stairs. Power to the building had been cut long ago to discourage students from crashing the place for parties. It was a nice idea, but it didn't work; I had chased my share of students out of the basement.

We ran up the steps, adrenaline giving us energy. I pushed open the door at the top and we stepped out into the sunshine, gasping for air.

I walked slowly toward the young man on the roof. He hadn't heard us enter and balanced precariously on the edge, staring at the crowd below.

"John, don't do this," Brie said.

The young man turned quickly and he wavered for a second as he fought to regain his balance, but he didn't step down. "Go away. I don't want anyone up here."

"What about your family? They love you. You can't do this to them," Brie pleaded.

"I can do what I want. It's my life," he retorted. His eyes were wide and jaw tight, the look of someone who felt he had no other choice. I had seen that look many times in the Arena.

"Just come down and talk. Please. For me?" Brie pleaded.

I took a step closer and shrugged my coat down one shoulder in case I needed to get it off quickly.

"Let's get off the roof and talk. What do you say?" Brie pressed.

John looked down at the ground far below us. "Okay," he agreed, his tone strange. He turned as if to step down, then gave Brie a small smile, opened his arms, and fell backward.

Brie screamed and I lunged for his hand, grabbing it just as he fell over the edge. His weight pulled me with him; we plummeted off the roof.

Brie cried my name. I fought to get my bearings and take off my coat. Shouts of surprise and shock rose from the crowd below. The wind rushed past like laughter in my ears, calling for me to open my wings and join its carefree dance. John flailed wildly; I struggled to hold him as I freed my other arm from the coat and let it flap away behind me. The crowd below sped quickly toward us. My heart raced. I wrapped my arms around John to stop his thrashing, then forced my wings open just before we hit the ground.

The wind caught my wings like a battering ram; my old scars burned in protest, but my wings held and I pushed them down hard. We skimmed over the top of the crowd. I let John go on a patch of grass, then crashed a few yards away on the hard ground. I rose slowly. My right wing throbbed. I didn't dare fly again. The crowd stared at me with wide eyes. Cell phones glinted in the rising sun and my heart slowed.

It was inevitable now. Students were already sending videos to their friends of what had happened. I glanced up and saw Dane standing on the edge of the crowd. He met my eyes and gave a triumphant smile, lifting his phone meaningfully. My heart dropped. With his help, the Academy would definitely find me. The crowd of students, parents, teachers, school faculty, and city workers who had surrounded the building made their way to John, and I felt everyone's eyes on my wings. I turned and stumbled past a building and into a shadowed alley.

Chapter Fourteen

"You shouldn't have done it," Jayce said, pacing the living room.

"You would have done the same thing," Nikko replied calmly.

"No, I wouldn't," Jayce protested.

"Oh, you're right," Nikko agreed. "Anyone with a normal heart would have. You, however, would have let John fall to his death."

"If it meant saving my hide, yes," Jayce replied, but there was doubt in his voice this time.

"It doesn't matter," Brie said. She leaned against my chest, her knees tucked up under her chin as she sat beside me on the couch. "What's done is done. We have to figure out what to do now."

"Kale needs to run." Jayce spoke as though I wasn't in the room.

"We can hide him here," Nikko said at the same time.

I shook my head, my voice calm despite the thoughts that tumbled through my mind. "I've got to let them take me."

All three of them turned to stare. Brie's eyes filled with tears. "Kale?"

I shook my head. "We knew it would happen eventually. We were crazy to believe otherwise. It's only going to be harder if we don't accept it." I glanced out the window at the night sky, amazed they hadn't found us already. In the back of my mind, a small thought reminded me that my security shift had started a few minutes ago. I wondered if Mr. Mason had found someone to take over.

"You promised," Brie said, her voice unsteady.

"I said if there was a way," I reminded her gently. "Now I've put us all in danger."

"John's put us all in danger," Jayce cut in. He cracked his knuckles. "I hope he knows the result of his stupid action."

Nikko touched his shoulder. "He knows," he reminded him quietly.

And he was right. John and his very grateful mother had come to the house earlier, some of the many people who had flocked discreetly to Dr. Ray's home in pairs and trios to talk about what they had witnessed and give us their encouragement. Several even offered me places to hide, but in the end they all left because they knew what would happen if they were near me when the guards came.

"But you can't just go," Jayce argued. "You've got to fight it. The system is wrong."

"Then we have to fight it at its source. None of us has power here," I said.

"The video's not done yet," Nikko argued. "It still needs work."

"And we need to wait until the Blood Match. It's imperative that we try to catch as many viewers as we can." My voice sounded more sure than I felt. "I'll be fine until then."

Brie pushed off the couch and left the room. My heart slowed at the sound of a door slamming shut.

I rose from the couch and put on my coat.

"Where are you going?" Nikko asked. Jayce just stared at me.

"I need to clear my head."

"What if they find you?"

"Better out there than here." I put a hand on both their shoulders, then went out the front door into the night.

***

I slid my fingers along the rough bricks of the library, remembering all the memories since the day Brie, Nikko, and Jayce had found me and given me a new life. The night air hung heavy with the scent of rain and a breeze ran teasingly through my hair, promising freedom if I took to the skies. Familiar footsteps sounded around the corner.

I looked back to see Jayce hurrying toward me through the mist that had settled over the city grounds like a protective blanket.

Jayce's hands clenched when he caught up. His eyes were dark and matched the tumultuous night. "What are you still doing here?"

I knew he wouldn't understand, but said it anyway. "I can't just leave."

The mist slowly turned into rain. Jayce peered through it at me. "You can't stay here. They'll find you."

The concern in his voice touched me. I remembered his hostility my first days at the house, and sighed silently at the difference our time together had made. "If I leave, they'll come down on all of you. You know that. It's better this way."

Jayce shook his head. "Nikko's hiding everything. There won't be any evidence at the house that you were there."

The thought was surprisingly painful. I turned away, but Jayce grabbed the front of my shirt. Adrenaline rushed through me and I fought down the impulse to flip him onto his back. "You can't go back, Kale. I can't see you dead on the Arena floor."

I stared at him. Rain dripped down my hair and into my eyes. I shook my head to clear it. "We knew this was coming.

Deep down, I think we all knew there was never a way to beat the system."

Jayce shoved me roughly. "Don't say that. Don't ever say that. There's a way; we have the way. The video's going to work. You just have to wait until it's ready."

The urgency in his voice grabbed my heart like a fist. I forced my voice past the knot in my throat. "This is the way, Jayce. I'm the only one who can fight from the inside."

He stared at me and his chest heaved. He held his hands at his sides and clenched and unclenched his fists. "So that's it? You're going to give up? You going to leave us, leave Brie, just like that?"

I fought down the urge to hit something as the anger I had pushed deep down at the situation threatened to rise up and take control. "You don't get it, Jayce. They know where I am, who I was with. If they don't find me, they'll come after you. Then you can all kiss your futures goodbye. They're relentless." The rain started to fall harder and I glared at him through it. "I've lived at the Academy my whole life. They'll never give up until they find me. Letting them come for me is the only way to protect you, Nikko, Dr. Ray, and Brie."

Jayce opened his mouth to argue, but he knew I spoke the truth. He shut his mouth and his jaw clenched, then he spun without a word and left back through the darkness. A pit rose in my stomach. I let the stress that had built up in my muscles fade with a slow breath. I forced my footsteps forward, continuing on my path.

My muscles tensed again at the sight of a form waiting for me next to the new city building, but when I drew closer, I saw that it was Mr. Mason. He turned silently at my approach. When I nodded at him, he fell in beside me.

"I didn't think you'd show and took over your rounds. You should be with your friends," he said quietly.

I shook my head. "It's not safe for them."

He nodded as we walked together. "That was a brave thing you did back there," he said after a few minutes.

"You would have done it, too," I replied.

He hesitated, then tipped his head pointedly toward my back. "If I'd had those, yeah, I probably would have."

I felt a little bit better and gave him a smile. "Thanks."

"I always knew you were different," he said after we had checked the doors to the utilities center and continued down the beat path.

"Really?" I questioned with raised eyebrows. I relished the feeling of the rain as it soaked through my coat.

He shrugged. "Not that I would have guessed how different. But it was the way you carried yourself. Confident, you know? Sure of yourself. Not something these guys have learned yet." He gestured vaguely toward the school grounds.

I looked away. "Not feeling so sure of myself right now," I admitted briefly.

He gave another nod. "I can believe it. I wouldn't blame you for not wanting to go back. I can't imagine what they do to make you guys fight like that."

I didn't answer and instead bent to check the chains around the doors at the front of one of the original settler's houses to hide my expression.

"It's okay to be scared, boy," he said gruffly.

I glanced at him and couldn't hide the shame I felt. He read it on my face.

"You're not the only one debating whether to run from a fight. I was a gunner once, and was tempted not to return from leave on more than one occasion." He took off his hat and for the first time I noticed the blaze of silver that ran through his otherwise brown hair. "That one nearly killed me." He put his hat back on and we continued on our path through the falling rain.

"What made you go back?" I finally asked.

He sighed. "It was my fight. You've got to pick your battles, the ones you can truly make a difference in." He glanced at me. "You know what I mean?" At my nod, he smiled. "You'll make the right choice. That doesn't mean it's always the easiest."

We walked on in silence; at the end of the beat, he patted my shoulder and walked away through the darkness. I listened until his footsteps faded away, then slid down the side of the library until I rested with my back against the cold bricks. I put my head on my knees and gave in to the tears.

They were tears of anger at a situation I didn't want to face, of fear at returning to life at the Academy, of heartache at leaving Brie, of loneliness so sharp it threatened to engulf me. Tears I had never allowed myself to cry mixed with the rain.

After several minutes had passed, I forced the pain back down. I allowed myself one wracking sob, then put the wall back up and once more locked up the emotions that could get me killed. I pushed up from the wall and stared into the rain. An achingly familiar figure stood near the library stairs.

"Brie?"

She pushed her hood back and let the rain fall on her face as she walked down the sidewalk. I couldn't tell if it was the chill of the rain or crying that made her nose and cheeks red, but the sight slowed my heart and made me want to go to her and hold her in my arms, to tell her everything was going to be alright. I forced myself to hold back. "You shouldn't be here. You can't be around when they find me."

She stopped a few feet away; the rain fell between us. "You're not spending your last free night alone."

I shook my head. "It's too dangerous, you've got to-"

She crossed the last few steps while I spoke and silenced me with a kiss. "I won't let them take this from me," she whispered when she pulled away. She took my hand and guided me to the back steps of the new city building. I sat on the stairs and she settled next to me, leaning against my shoulder.

I memorized the profile of her face against the lights inside the doors, and breathed in her scent as though it was the last thing I would ever smell. She took one of my hands and gently traced the scars along the back. "You're not going to be safe in there," she whispered.

I rested my chin on top of her head. "I wasn't exactly safe out here," I replied.

She gave a soft sigh and turned my hand over to run her fingers along my palm. I closed my eyes and enjoyed just feeling her touch and the love that flowed from it. "We should fight them," she said.

I shook my head. "This is the only way. We knew it would come to this eventually."

She sat up and met my gaze. "But is it too soon?"

I willed my heart to slow at the pleading in her eyes. "I'll be alright," I said, forcing myself to sound unconcerned.

She frowned slightly. "I don't believe you."

I gave her a small smile. "I'd rather you think of me safe, then worry about things you can't control."

She thought about it for a minute, then sighed again. "I can't help but worry."

I brushed a stray strand of hair from her face and twirled it around my fingers. "Will you do me one thing?" I asked quietly.

"What?"

I studied the hair between my fingers to avoid meeting her eyes. "Don't try to stop them when they come to get me."

I felt her eyes on me. "I've got to," she said honestly.

I shook my head and looked down at her. "It'll make it that much harder for me to go and someone could get hurt. We both know I have to do this. If I go quietly, it'll be better for everyone." I held her gaze. "Will you do that for me?"

Tears filled her soft brown eyes again, but she blinked them back and nodded. "Yes." She buried her head against my chest and I held her tight, fearing every second that brought us closer to being apart. I counted each breath and memorized the way her hair fell over her shoulders. She eventually fell asleep in my arms. I traced her cheek softly, hoping my fingers would remember the touch of her skin after I returned to the brutality of the Academy. I held her close and watched the dawn rise slowly out of the darkest night I could remember.

***

Brie, Nikko, Jayce, and I entered Dr. Ray's classroom together. Talking abruptly ceased and all eyes turned to us. I made my way to my regular chair near the back of the classroom with Brie at my arm.

"Kale?"

I turned to see Dr. Ray walk through the door.

"Yes, sir?"

"Come here."

I glanced at Brie; she watched Dr. Ray in uncertainty. We hadn't spoken since our conversation on the city building steps the night before. There was nothing else to say between us but lingering gazes and the touch of fingertips. Love beat so strongly in my chest that my heart threatened to burst free. I knew it would break the second I walked out the door and out of Brie's life. But for now, I gave her a reassuring smile and went back up to the front of the classroom.

"You needn't wear this any longer," Dr. Ray said. Without waiting for an answer, he helped me out of my coat and tossed it toward the garbage can near the door. It landed in a heap on the ground. He gave me a sharp nod. "Be proud of who you are. We're proud of you."

Several students nodded and smiled at me as I made my way back to my desk. I sat down, feeling exposed and liberated at the same time. Dr. Ray could get in a lot of trouble if the authorities showed up and realized he had known I was Galdoni. The thought that he dared let me show it in his classroom filled me with a kind of proud wonder.

Dr. Ray was a few minutes into his lecture when the door burst open and ten armed guards shoved their way through. Dane stood triumphantly next to the head guard. He gave me a wicked grin.

185

"I'm teaching a class here," Dr. Ray told them calmly.

"Silence," a guard with a black armband commanded. "We've come to take KL426 back to the Academy where he belongs."

"He belongs here," Dr. Ray stated in the same even tone. Several students chuckled at the look of frustration on the guard's face. The guard turned and scanned the students with an impatient gaze. His eyes fell on me and widened slightly. He took a step in my direction.

"He's a student," Steven, one of Zach's friends from the party, said. He rose and blocked the aisle to my desk.

"Yeah," Brandi, a girl who was also in my economics class, seconded. She rose to stand behind him.

A red-headed boy stood wordlessly behind her, and others followed until every student in the room grouped in front of my desk. Their actions threatened to break my careful composure.

"Get out of our way or we'll make you move," the head guard threatened. He lifted his gun.

My heart beat loudly in my chest, but I forced down any show of emotion. "It's okay; let them through."

Several of the students glanced back at me. Steven met my eyes and shook his head. I nodded and he reluctantly stepped back. The head guard gave a grim smile and pushed his way past them to my desk.

"KL426?" he demanded.

"My name is Kale," I stated firmly.

He lifted his gun threateningly, anger evident on his face. I merely smiled. "If you're coming to arrest a person, you'd better make sure you have the right name."

The students around me gave small laughs, but the guard glowered. "You're not a person, you're a Galdoni and a threat

186

to these students. I am under orders to take you off these premises immediately. Resistance will be punished by death."

"Then I'd better not resist," I said, my tone heavily laced with sarcasm.

The guard glared at me, uncertain whether I had agreed to come with him or not. I rose and he took an involuntary step back. I gave a grim smile. "Lead the way, oh fearless escort."

Students mocked him as we walked to the front of the room. I looked back and caught Brie's eyes. 'I love you', I mouthed, and then was shoved roughly out the door.

Chapter Fifteen

My welcome back to the Academy was about what I had expected. The guards led me through the gates that I had hoped to never enter again, across the cement courtyard, through the giant, four-inch-thick metal doors, and into my old cell where they attached my handcuffs to a chain hanging from the ceiling and proceeded to beat me to within an inch of my life, which hurt a lot more than I remembered.

When they finally released the chains and let me collapse on the floor, I curled in on my broken ribs and bruised organs. Even breathing hurt. Images of Brie and my life at school felt like a dream, but a dream I wanted to return to more than anything. Pain throbbed from every inch of my body, but as I felt the ache of familiar scars, I blocked out all other thoughts but the memory of gentle hands tending to my wounds, soft laughter around a familiar table, and the scent of lavender shampoo in the rain. I fell into a merciful sleep several hours later with Brie's name on my lips.

CHEREE ALSOP

***

The sound of a plate being shoved through the slot in the door woke me. All I could think of was *no, no, no. Not here. Don't let me be here.* I finally forced my eyes open and saw the cold gray walls and iron door that had been my home for most of my life.

Not home, I reminded myself. *Home was with Brie, and with Nikko, Jayce, and Dr. Ray. This will never be home.*

I sat up slowly, holding my ribs against the sharp ache that stole my breath. Blood caked the side of my face from a gash above my eyebrow. I felt it gingerly. It was about an inch below the one Dr. Ray had sewn. I remembered Brie's soft voice upon finding me awake the first time. I took a shallow breath to keep futile tears from burning my eyes.

Then I remembered the cameras. I glanced up at the corner of the room where a tiny security camera had been recessed behind a thick plate of glass. I wondered if they could see me. The way Iggy and the others had perused the database, I knew it wouldn't be hard to find my cell. I pictured Brie watching me the way we had the young Galdoni boy while he stared at nothing. I shook my head. She wouldn't see me like that. Now I was living for her.

I pushed off the pallet that made a sorry excuse for a bed and rose slowly to my feet. I stretched, pretending not to feel the sharp pain of the gashes across my chest from the guards' hungry whips, or the bruises that covered my back and wings, bringing to life the pain of my old scars and what would be many new ones. I grabbed the plate from the floor and ate the meager crusty bread and mystery meat like it was one of Brie's sandwiches. After drinking the stale water that had been shoved in a dirty bowl after the food, I got to work. There was a lot to do, and I wasn't in any shape to do it yet.

189

I began with push-ups, reminding my sore muscles what they used to be used for before I went to school. Lying back on the floor to do crunches with my wings out opened up the crusted gashes across my chest, so I did them shallowly and concentrated instead on the burn of the muscles across my stomach. I then picked up my pallet and leaned it against the wall like I had done so many thousands of times before. I wrapped my knuckles in the pitiful, dirty blankets that barely deserved the name, and proceeded to pound my frustrations out on the boards.

My body fell into its old cadence; my muscles remembered the punches, blocks, spins, kicks, and ducks that I used to practice every day until they came as naturally as breathing. In the Academy, instinct was life, and my body hadn't forgotten.

But with each hit, the memories of school and Brie and the others felt more and more like a dream, a dream so good I wished to curl up on the same battered pallet and fall back into it, but a dream just the same. With every block, I fought to keep Brie's face in my mind, her beautiful brown eyes and perfumed hair, the way she touched my arm when we talked quietly on the porch, and the feeling of her head against my chest when she dozed under my arm. Most of all, I remembered the brush of her lips against mine, the sweetness of her kiss, and the way her soft smile lit up any room like summer.

I didn't let myself wonder whether I would ever see her again. This was the Academy, and here we lived to die. I didn't know if the video would work, but maybe it would give Brie hope so she wouldn't waste her precious days worrying about me. Whether I lived or died in the Arena would be up to me, and I had a plan.

***

"Well, well, if it isn't KL426," a guard scoffed as I made my way down the secure hallway to the mess hall.

"My name's Kale," I responded casually; I braced for the anger I knew would follow.

"Are you talking to me?" the guard bellowed. He hit me with his club across the shoulders hard enough to make me stumble forward. But I regained my balance and kept walking as though nothing had happened. "Stupid beasts, coming back thinking they have names and such," he muttered to his fellow guard. His voice rose. "I don't care what happened out there, but you're less than animals in here, and it's best if you remember it!" His voice echoed down the hall and several other guards laughed.

The other Galdoni around me avoided meeting my eyes as we turned into the mess hall and found our assigned tables. Security had increased a great deal since I had been gone. Instead of getting our own meals, we waited at the tables and the meals were brought to us. "Like being served at a restaurant," I whispered with a chuckle.

Several Galdoni lifted their heads to stare at me, and one even gave a small smile of surprise, but they dropped their eyes when a pair of guards walked between the tables.

I pretended to study my food, but stole glances around the room. I estimated one hundred and fifty Galdoni from my age group, about twenty-five short from before we left the Academy. I recognized most of them, having practiced against them for when we would fight to the death; I wouldn't consider any of them a friend. After a few harrowing experiences in friendship during childhood that usually ended in life-threatening beatings and sometimes death, we had learned to avoid each other.

So when I tapped on the arm of the Galdoni next to me after the guard had passed, I wasn't surprised at the look of shock on his face. The Galdoni was huge, hulking, brown-winged, and a few years older than I. I had fought him a few times in practice, and knew he hit like a battering ram. A scar traced down the left side of his face, causing his lip to twist down in a frightening scowl. He glared at me, then turned back to eating the gray gruel that tasted more like paste than food.

I waited for the guards' next round, then tapped his arm again.

"What?" he growled quietly in a tone laced with menace.

"How long were you out?" I asked, pretending not to hear the threat.

He stared at me for a second, then shook his head. "You're crazy." He turned back to his meal.

I pursed my lips and slid my plate closer to his. He glanced over at me again suspiciously. "You're a big guy, bigger than me, and this food doesn't even touch my hunger. I can't imagine how you must feel. Don't you hate going hungry every day?" His gaze darkened, but I took it as a good sign that he continued to listen. "Tell you what. You can have my food if you just talk to me."

The guards came by again and he turned away. I was about to pull my plate back, but he put a finger on it after the guards had passed. "We talk, I eat?" he asked quietly, his eyes still full of suspicion.

"That's it," I answered with a nod.

He considered for a moment, then slid his empty plate to me and pulled mine in front of him. He took a bite of the cold gruel. "Six months."

"What?"

He glanced at me, exasperated. "I was out six months before they caught me."

I wondered how a Galdoni so huge could have hidden for so long. He caught my stare and shrugged. "I found a job as a bouncer. It was dark. I liked it."

I fought back a smile at his simple words. There was weight behind them, longing. "I came back last week. I went to school."

He let out a surprised chuckle, deep like the growl of a lion. Several others glanced at me, too. "School? Didn't you get enough schooling here?" He ducked as the guards passed again.

I waited for them to get out of earshot. "I learned about real stuff, not the filtered crap the Academy teaches us. I learned about anatomy, and about language and history and economics."

"Not our history," a Galdoni across from us shot back. He glowered at his plate as though daring the gruel to get away.

"Some of our history," I replied. "We *are* part human."

The Galdoni next to him scoffed. "Yeah, right. We saw how the humans welcomed us."

A whip cracked above our heads. "No talking!" the guard shouted.

We fell silent for the next several passes, then I took a steeling breath. "We found our places, and I have a plan for a better reception next time if we can survive in here."

Despite their fear of the guards, several more Galdoni down the table looked at me expectantly. "A plan?" the huge Galdoni next to me grunted. He finished my meal and put an enormous elbow on the table. Plates rattled.

"I have friends on the outside, human friends." At their annoyed looks, I smiled. "It is possible. I know I'm not the only one to have made friends out there."

I saw a few nods of agreement around the table. A skinny Galdoni with light brown wings and red hair who sat on the other side of the giant met my eyes. "Do you really think we could go back?" His eyes held hope and fear.

I nodded. "Definitely. If we play our cards right."

"What do we have to do?" the Galdoni across from me asked, his dark eyes guarded.

I shrugged and smiled at the thought of my conversation with Zach. "It's simple. Not fight."

Several of them laughed, and they all turned away from me. Whispers rose that I was insane. I was losing them, and didn't know how to get them back.

"Listen to him," the big Galdoni next to me growled quietly. The others fell silent. "At least he has a plan," he muttered. A few glanced at me.

I took the opportunity. "Look, we all know we're here because our fights bring money to the gamblers. So what do we do? We wait until the Blood Match and then refuse to fight in the Arena. What can they do to us?"

"Kill us," someone at the table behind me piped in.

I shook my head. "We're too valuable. That's why they brought us back instead of killing us before. They need us."

Everyone fell silent for the next few guard passes.

Finally, the big Galdoni next to me grunted again. "We don't fight. People can't gamble. Then what?"

I smiled. "Then my guys on the outside work their magic."

At the end of lunch, the big Galdoni told me I could call him Goliath, the name he had given himself when he left the

Academy. I stifled a laugh when the skinny red-head told me his name was David.

"Like the Bible?"

They both nodded. "We were roommates out there," David explained. He elbowed the big Galdoni. "And he needed a protector."

A rare smile appeared on Goliath's face; he didn't disagree.

Later, I found myself practicing next to the big Galdoni in the weapons combat room.

"What happens if Galdoni fight anyway?" Goliath asked between swings; he proceeded to bash apart a large wooden dummy with a mace.

"It'll undermine what I'm trying to do. We need everyone to be on the same page." I weaved the broadsword I was holding in a figure eight to warm up my shoulders.

"No talking," a guard yelled. He cracked his whip and the sting of the lash caught me just behind my left ear. I gritted my teeth and tried to ignore the trickle of blood that made its way down my neck. I threw my anger into the sword and swung it as hard as I could at the dummy suspended in front of me. The blade cut cleanly through the canvas middle. I spun back around with the momentum and sliced through the dummy's neck as well.

A guard came out grumbling about wasting perfectly good dummies as he replaced the one I had mutilated with one less damaged. He glanced at me; surprise showed on his face when he met my angry gaze. He glared back in an effort to hide the glint of fear that showed in his eyes. "You know broad swords are for the wooden dummies. See that you follow the rules or I'll report you." He stomped off in loud bravado, towing the mangled dummy behind him.

Goliath gave a soft chuckle. "Remind me not to get on your bad side."

I fought back a smile. "I thought the same thing about you in the lunchroom."

He turned away before we were noticed, then he grinned and tore through my fresh dummy with his mace.

The guard that had just replaced it gave a strangled yell and I wove through rows of fighters toward the wooden dummies before he could accuse me of starting anything.

"Hey, you!" he yelled behind me.

I ducked my head and took a few more steps only to find my way blocked by another guard. "He's talking to you, Galdoni," he said, spitting the last word like it left a bad taste in his mouth.

I glanced back over my shoulder as though I hadn't noticed the shouting, red faced guard. I made my way back to him, the broadsword resting casually across one shoulder. The room fell silent. "Yes, sir?"

He pointed at the destroyed dummy. "Did you do this?"

I shook my head with an exaggeratedly baffled expression. "No, sir. I only have a sword. It wouldn't do that kind of damage." I hefted the sword to prove my point, and he ducked as though afraid I was going to cut off his head. Several chuckles sounded around us, but when the guard cracked his whip, they returned to their activities.

"I think you had something to do with this," he said, his eyebrows low over menacing black eyes.

I shrugged. "Why would I? I was on my way to the wooden dummies like you suggested."

"Suggested?" he sputtered. "Ordered, more like it." He glanced at one of the other guards, unsure what to do. The other guard gave a small shrug, clearly just as interested as the Galdoni at what his next move would be.

The guard's face grew even redder. "Get in the holding box."

"On what charge?" Normally, I wouldn't question such an order, but I was feeling overly unruly.

The guard looked as though he was going to explode. He sputtered again, searching for the right words, then shouted, "I don't have to explain myself to you!"

I shrugged as though I couldn't care less and turned to go.

"Give me that!" he demanded.

I glanced back to see him hold out his hand for my sword. With a small smile, I brought it down from my shoulder and switched my grip so that he could grasp the hilt. I let go and turned away just before he could get a good grip. I didn't look back at the sound of the blade hitting the ground followed by a series of very detailed expletives. A few Galdoni stared at me as I made my way to the door, and a couple of the older ones even smiled. I pushed open the door and casually pulled the fire alarm on my way down the hall.

Chapter Sixteen

I was careful not to be the first one in the Arena as guards herded the Galdoni in and then left to investigate the source of the alarm. I stretched my wings, but only glanced at the false sky of the Arena dome. I wasn't the only one who refused to enjoy the brief seconds of flight the Arena offered. It wasn't freedom, not now that we had tasted what it meant to truly fly. Several other Galdoni glared at the dome, while most of us ignored it entirely.

"What are we waiting for?" someone in the back grumbled.

"Better hurry; you don't have much time." I turned to find Goliath at my side, David next to him. The big Galdoni grinned. "Allow me." He cleared his throat and then roared, "Brothers, Kale has a message he needs to share and we've got to hurry, so quiet down and listen. It might mean your freedom."

"Freedom?"

"False hope."

"What's he talking about?"

I ignored the mutters and gestured toward the dome. "You know we're captives here. If our taste of freedom did anything, it gave us a thirst for life beyond these walls." Several half-hearted agreements met my words, but they died away quickly at the skepticism on the faces of their comrades.

"We don't have much time," I continued, "But I have a plan to get us out of here."

"They aren't going to let us go," a small Galdoni who was missing several fingers argued.

"They'll have to if we don't bring them a profit," I pointed out.

"They profit when we die," someone stated helpfully.

198

I gave him a small smile. "Exactly, so we don't die."

Mutters rose, but quieted down when Goliath glared at them.

"And how do you propose we do that?" the small Galdoni asked.

I shrugged. "It's simple. We don't fight."

This time, the laughter that followed was harder to silence. I knew we were running out of time, so I didn't wait. "Brothers, if we don't fight, they have nothing to gamble on and no one makes money. Without money, the Academy falls."

There was more grumbling, but looks of comprehension also dawned on many faces. "He's right," I heard one Galdoni say to his neighbors.

"What's our motto here?" I asked.

"Fight with honor, fight-"

I shook my head. "Not the Academy's motto for us, but our own motto?"

A Galdoni with gray hair and many scars stepped forward and turned beside me so that he faced the others. ""This is the Academy, and here we live to die." The words had been scratched into the floor of holding cell two, one of the most used cells for isolation. I didn't know who originally put them there, but over the years the words had been traced by the rotation of occupants until they were etched so deep the stones would have to be removed to erase them.

I nodded. "I used to believe that we were dying for honor, for glory, for a greater cause, because that's what *they* would have us believe." I gestured toward the sound of feet marching down the hall toward the Arena. "But the truth, which you already know, is that we are dying to fill the pockets of men eager for our blood to be spilled. We are dying for mere entertainment. Is that a worthy cause?"

I didn't expect an answer, but shouts of 'No' echoed through the Arena. A feral grin stretched across my face. "Are we going to let them win?"

"No!" they yelled louder.

"Then stand with me. Don't slay your brethren for *their* monetary gain. Together, we can beat this!"

A roar of approval echoed off the Arena walls. My heart sang with it until a black-haired, gray-winged Galdoni stepped forward. The gathered Galdoni hushed at the sight of him and the other four Galdoni that stepped forward.

"Yes, Blade?" He was one of the few who had won so many battles he had been allowed to pick a name that was recognized by the Academy.

Blade gave me a cruel smile. "And what if we want to fight, little one?" he asked, mocking my lack of fights in the Arena.

I glared at him. "Then you destroy our chance to leave here."

His grin grew wider and more pointed. "And you think they'd just let you leave?" he asked, his tone incredulous. "You think that if you refused to fight and cost *them* millions, they'd just hand you the keys to the gate and let you walk away?" He laughed and his followers echoed it.

"As if," one said. Blade glared at him and he shut his mouth.

Blade shook his head and dropped the false, light tone. When he spoke again, his voice was deep and menacing. "Let me tell you something." He stepped closer so that we were almost toe to toe. "I'm fighting in the Arena, and I hope it's your puny body I get to crush beneath my mace."

My muscles tensed at the hatred and venom in his voice, but I forced myself to hold still. "I don't care if you throw away your own life or even mine, but don't destroy the only chance the rest of them have."

He gave another cruel smile and then spit in my face. I lost my carefully reined control and was about to swing at him when the doors burst open and guards with whips and night sticks ran through to encircle the Galdoni.

"Enough talking," the lead guard said; his eyes swept past us as though we were below the value of bugs and barely worth his notice. "Someone pulled the alarm. No dinner or breakfast, and you'll be doing drills all day tomorrow."

Several Galdoni protested, but the lash of whips ended any talking.

"Get to your cells and don't make another sound," the guard snapped as though talking to a group of disobedient dogs. "Or I'll just shoot you and claim self-defense." He laughed. No one would be held accountable for the death of a mere Galdoni. He turned away, chuckling at his own joke.

"Someone needs to teach that man a lesson," a Galdoni behind me muttered as we were herded out of the Arena like a bunch of sheep.

"And you're going to do it?" the Galdoni next to him stated. They both fell silent at the crack of a whip just above their heads.

We walked slowly to our cells, Galdoni breaking away when we passed their blocks. I was almost to mine when a hand touched my wing. "Did you really mean what you said back there?"

I glanced back to see a black and white winged Galdoni a few years younger than me. At least five others with him waited for my answer. I nodded. "It's the way out of here, and it will work."

"What if Blade fights?" he pressed anxiously.

201

My stomach clenched, but I said the truth. "Then I'll kill him. No one will stand in the way of our freedom."

***

I sat on my pallet with my head in my hands after a particularly brutal beating for pulling the alarm and also for 'conspiring', even though they apparently had no idea what was said during our little gathering. Thoughts and images of Brie swirled through my weary mind. I could keep them at bay during the training and grind of the day, but being alone in a cell brought them back with a force strong enough to take my breath away.

I saw Brie's eyes, beautiful and kind, the color of mahogany with a hint of gold encircling the irises. I saw my own reflection in her eyes, and wondered why she cared about someone like me, a nobody Galdoni destined to die. I hated myself for letting her care. I knew at the beginning that it would end in the Arena, and I shouldn't have let her know my true feelings; I was so in love with her that every second away tore at my heart with a thousand daggers.

I fought to keep the emotions at bay, to pretend that my life out there didn't exist. It felt like a dream so much that I wanted it to be; the freedom and life I had experienced there was more than someone like me could have ever hoped for. But then I would hear the echo of her laugh, feel the light touch of her hand on my arm, smell the whisper of her scent on the air, and it was all I could do to keep from falling apart.

I knew they watched me. That night I turned to the camera. "I will come back to you, Brie," I promised. "I love you." I held her eyes, knowing she watched me the way I would have never let her leave my sight if she was the one behind the glass. I then settled on the pallet and let sleep steal the pain from my body in the same way that dreams of Brie eased the pain of my soul.

***

The next day, I dedicated myself to fighting whole-heartedly. I didn't know if I would be fighting Blade or any of his minions, but I wanted to be ready. I didn't believe for a second that the Academy would let us get away with not fighting. I would have to be prepared to defend the other Galdoni if it came down to that.

The Galdoni around me whispered questions and passed information back and forth. I became the one they told of their secret lives outside the Academy doors. Everyone had a story, a hope, a dream, something they wished to return to or try if they ever got out again. Listening to them made my own dreams ache with even more intensity, but I listened because it gave them hope.

"I danced," one particularly large Galdoni whispered as he released me from a choke hold and shoved me back against the ropes. I fought to hide an incredulous smile when I spun back to face him. He was even bigger than Goliath, or at least his twin in size, but the light in his eyes told of a desire for the stage, for grace and beauty and all the things that didn't exist behind the Academy gates.

"I cooked fillet mignon with mushrooms drenched in a beef broth and cream sauce," the skinny, tall Galdoni who would have fit the image of a scholar had he been human told me before he spun left in an attempt to hack off my arm with his sword. "The vegetables were delectable, grated and cooked until they were soft but still crisp."

I vaulted a brick wall and landed beside a small Galdoni with gray and white wings in the training yard. "Snowboarding," he said as we jumped over a low vault and scrambled up a rope ladder.

"What?" I asked, gasping for air.

"There's nothing like the hiss of snow under your board and the feeling of the flakes as they race past your face." He ducked under a running bridge and jumped the next vault. "I felt so alive."

"You'll be alive again," I promised him as I dodged spinning dummies with real blades.

"You really think not fighting will work?" he wheezed when we reached the end of the course. He bent over with his hands on his knees to catch his breath.

I nodded, taking in huge gulps of air. I didn't mention that it was our only hope, or that it would probably be the only attempt they would give me before guards killed me as an example to the rest. In my mind, it just had to work.

Chapter Seventeen

"Kill me now, weakling," Blade taunted behind his serrated sword.

He lunged and I parried, dancing back beyond his reach. His sword caught mine across the middle and snapped right through my blade; his next lunge barely missed my stomach. It wasn't the first time that I suspected they gave Blade better weapons in the hopes that he would use the advantage to kill me. Only through sheer will and speed did I manage to make it out of the matches alive. I threw my half blade at him and glanced aside to see two guards by the door exchange money.

That angered me more than Blade's superior weapons. I growled and ducked under Blade's next move, a showy swing for the amusement of the Galdoni who had stopped fighting practice to watch us.

He grunted when I caught him around the middle and forced him back against the chains. He beat my head with the hilt of his sword, but couldn't bring the large weapon around to reach me. I ignored the battering and punched him as hard as I could with a left, then a right. Though he wore protective padding, I could hear the air that was forced from his lungs. I threw another right and felt a satisfying snap as his ribs gave way.

Blade surprised me with a left foot sweep. I stumbled back, but managed to keep on my feet. He took advantage of the stumble to lunge again with his sword. I fell back a second too slow and the blade cut through my padding and bit into my chest.

Blade grinned wildly and lunged again, but I was ready. I grasped the blade between my palms, careful to keep my fingers free of the cutting edge, and fell backward. The movement threw him off balance and he fell with me. I twisted as I hit the ground. The tip of the sword drove into the cement floor inches from my side. Blade let out a huff of air as the hilt jammed painfully into his stomach. He fell to the side, gasping. I rolled back to my feet and picked up the sword, then put the tip to his throat.

"Hold it!" one of the guards called out. He pushed through the crowd of eager Galdoni, many of whom urged me with little nods and gestures to end Blade's life and relieve us of his constant bullying. I wanted to kill him, to end his life as badly as I had wanted to end Brie's step-father's. The promise of bloodshed whispered through the stale air, and the wound across my chest ached for retaliation. My vision tinged in red.

I debated for a brief second. With Blade gone, there would be few others who would dare to go against us and fight in the Arena. A quote from one of the religious theory books a professor had let me borrow in secret came to mind. 'It is better then that one man perish than a whole nation dwindle in unbelief.' I had seen the sense of it at the time, but now that the decision was mine, I hesitated. What right did I have to choose, and how would Blade's death make me any better than the gamblers who thirsted for our blood?

Before the guards could reach me with their whips and clubs, far too late for them to have stopped me anyway, I dropped the sword and walked away. I couldn't believe how close I had come to becoming the animal we were made out to be. The blood pounded in my ears, the thirst to kill rushing hot through my veins. I crossed blindly over the ropes and walked to a corner of the Arena. I sat on the padded floor and held my aching head in my hands. A trickle of blood flowed from a gash in my hair from Blade's hilt, but I ignored it.

A few minutes later, the sounds of training resumed. I forced down the blood thirsty adrenaline that pounded in my veins and fought to regain what I had thought was my humanity and self-control.

"Here, drink."

I lifted my head to see a pair of gnarled, stained hands offer me a cup of water. I almost pushed it away, but thirst burned in the back of my throat and I was reminded with an ache of when I met Brie, afraid to trust someone I couldn't see, the brush of her hand the only gentle thing I had ever felt.

I drank the water and set the cup aside. A glance at the bearer showed a Galdoni I knew by sight but had never spoken to. He was one of the oldest, a veteran of the Arena covered in the scars of battle. He gave a wry smile and sat down in front of me. It was then that I noticed the droop in his left wing from a break that hadn't been set right. My gut clenched when I realized that he could no longer fly.

"You should have killed him," the Galdoni said amiably. He stretched out his left leg slowly like it pained him.

"I know," I replied.

"Why didn't you? Honor?"

I snorted in disgust. "There's no honor here."

He gave me another slight smile. "You did just prove yourself wrong, you know."

I grimaced. "It wasn't honor that kept me from killing him. I didn't want to turn into the monster the humans make us out to be."

He glanced over his shoulder. "They don't have to try very hard," he said gently.

I followed his gaze and studied the room of grunting, yelling, cursing Galdoni who grappled, sword fought, and sparred like lions defending their pride. I sighed and rubbed my eyes. "Maybe the humans are right to keep us out of their society."

The older Galdoni shrugged. "Who says it's *their* society? We're alive, which means we have a place in it."

I gave a humorless laugh. "Not if they have any say in the matter."

He frowned at me then, his gray eyes studying mine. "Then you lied to them? You really don't think it's worth getting out of here?"

I pushed my palm against the side of my head in an effort to close the wound that continued to drip. "I don't know anymore. Out there," I gestured vaguely toward the walls, "It seemed so straightforward, so simple. We'd been wronged, and we deserved a chance to live our own lives."

When I fell silent, he pressed, "And now?"

I took a steeling breath. "And now sometimes I see us the way they do. We were raised this way. Can we really change?"

He patted me on the shoulder and pushed himself slowly to his feet. "Anyone can change, Kale. And everyone deserves the chance to do so." His voice lowered so no one could overhear us. "They'll fight for you, boy. Or not fight, as the case may be. The Galdoni need a leader and they look up to you. Lead them the right way and you might really pull this off."

He turned and walked away before I could come up with a reply.

Chapter Eighteen

Goliath sat by me in the cafeteria along with several other Galdoni who had started seeking us out wherever we went. It felt strange to have a following, but comforting to know that I wasn't the only one who felt like we had to stand up for ourselves. Goliath was silent while we ate, but I didn't think about it until David came running into the lunchroom.

"Kale, Kale, I'm so sorry!" he sobbed. He ran straight to our table and fell into a heap at my feet. I stared at him in shock. His shirt was missing and his chest and arms were covered in whip marks that streamed blood. His back already bore purpling bruises that would be nearly black by the time they were fully formed.

"What happened?" I asked. I fought to keep my voice calm. Goliath crouched next to him, a hulking giant towering over the tiny red-headed Galdoni.

"They beat me." His voice quivered. "I had to tell them. They would have killed me. I'm sorry, Kale."

A pit formed in my stomach at the fear in his voice. "What did you tell them?"

He put his face in his hands. "About not fighting. They heard that you pulled the fire alarm to organize some sort of rebellion, and they tortured me until I told them about it. They're coming for you."

Everyone had fallen silent at David's entrance. I glanced up and spotted Blade across the room. He met my eyes, his own carefully expressionless, then he and his followers returned to their eating.

"You should kill me. Kill me now," David pleaded.

I reached out. Goliath moved as if to stop me, but at my glance he backed down. I set a hand on David's shoulder. It trembled under my touch. "I won't hurt you," I promised him quietly. "Look at me." When he refused to look up, I softened my tone. "David, look at me brother."

He glanced up and tear marks trailed through the blood on his face.

"I don't blame you. You did the right thing. It's okay." I waited until he nodded, then I rose and stepped onto the table. The chain around my ankle rattled against the hard surface.

"Of course they'll try to stop us," I said, lifting my voice so it echoed around the room. I felt the eyes of one hundred and fifty Galdoni watching me. "They don't want you to be free, to live your own lives. But you deserve every second of it."

I glanced around the room, meeting as many eyes as I could. "You deserve to feel the wind in your wings, to smell the cool ocean breeze, to feel grass under your feet and the rain in your hair. You deserve these things, and they know it."

"Get down!" a guard yelled from across the room.

I clenched a fist. "Do you know why they treat us like animals? Because if they admit that we are part human, then they'll also have to admit they're being inhumane." I raised the fist into the air. "But you deserve better, and don't let them convince you otherwise. You live, you breathe, you dream the same as me, and the same as them. Outside of these walls there's a life out there waiting for each of us." A few Galdoni by the back wall rose to their feet, listening.

The guards in the lunchroom tried to reach me, but Galdoni stepped in front of them, blocking their path.

I held out my wings, gaining strength from the eagerness on their faces. "Prove to them that you're not animals. Don't fight at the Blood Match. My friends on the outside are working to free you, to undermine this system that is based

211

on lies. Don't fight, and let them see that we are not the animals they've tried to turn us into."

Fifteen armed guards burst through the mess hall doors. They swarmed the table where I stood, pushing Galdoni out of the way with their sticks and whips. I glanced at Blade one more time. He met my eyes with a sneer. 'I'll fight,' he mouthed.

I opened my mouth to retaliate, but a guard swept my legs out from under me with a nightstick and I landed hard on my back on the table. They beat me with their clubs. I didn't resist when they hauled me out of the cafeteria. The faint hope that my own lack of aggression might fuel the Galdoni who had listened was the last thought in my mind before they threw me into solitary confinement.

***

I realized while waiting in the cell that they would make me fight no matter what, unless I was willing to just lie down and die. An unfair death match would be the best way to get rid of me, and one that would be profitable for the Academy. Brie's pleading eyes came to my mind and I rubbed my bruised face. I wasn't willing to just lie down and die.

I rolled my shoulders to ease the ache left from the most recent beating. It had been several days since the cafeteria, and I was still in solitary with no sign of being let out. Hard bread, bits of old meat, and occasionally a piece of dried fruit or moldy cheese were shoved through the door slot along with a deluge of water that went straight to the floor if I forgot to leave my bucket in the right place. I was beaten occasionally, but ignored for the most part.

The obvious plan was to leave me in solitary until the Blood Match. I wouldn't have the chance to train, and I would be put in the first round as an example to the others. I wouldn't be given a true chance to fight, and whether I tried to or not, I would be killed by other Galdoni who were willing to stay, who thirsted for the kill. The realization solidified. I would be killed by Blade and his minions. It would completely destroy everything I had been trying to accomplish.

I rose and walked the seven feet to the far wall. The line of light that came through the side of the door fell a foot short of the ceiling which brushed the top of my head if I stood on my tiptoes. My wingspan full out was roughly eight feet, and my wings ached to stretch to their full length. I put a hand on the cold brick wall and debated my response to their scheme.

213

The solitary confinement cell was too small to be an efficient training room, but I had to make it work. The Blood Match was in less than a month, but I could lose a great deal of muscle and strength by then, especially on my current diet and if I stopped training completely. I put my back to the wall and surveyed my dark cell.

The camera was in its usual place behind thick glass in a corner where the ceiling met the wall. I put a hand on the glass, picturing Brie's face, the worry in her eyes, the pain in her smile, pain I had caused because I loved her.

"I love you, Brie," I whispered. "Trust me. Everything is going to be okay."

I tore a piece of the worn sheet that served as my only blanket and forced it between the caulked edge and the glass. It would keep Brie and the others from seeing me, which I regretted, but it would also prevent the guards from watching me train. It wouldn't be long before they realized I had caught on to their little plan, but I would do what I could in the meantime.

I had little to work with. There was no bed. The sheet wadded in the corner made up my sleeping quarters. I had a bucket for water, a bucket for waste, and the dim light that came through one side of the heavy metal door for nine hours a day from the hallway beyond. After that, it was the pitch black of a cave deep in the earth. I could prop the flap over the door slot open for a bit more light during the day, but it only made a slight difference.

I sat in the middle of the floor and turned to face one of the corners so that I could stretch my wings. It was the only way I had found where I could draw them out to their full length, and it felt good to stretch them after such a long confinement. I then proceeded to map out an exercise program that would keep my muscles from weakening.

The walls were just wide enough that, stretched out, I could put my feet on one side and use my hands on the other side to lift myself off the floor. I got to where I could move myself all the way up the wall to the ceiling and back down, and then I learned to do it with my back to the floor. I did hundreds of crunches, pushups, sit-ups, stretches, and yoga exercises to keep my body limber, then I turned to cardiovascular training.

I created an intensive workout of hand-to-hand combat techniques and kickboxing mixed with Chinese scrapping. The result was a rigorous fighting workout that honed my skills in close combat.

I had always excelled at weapons arts, leaving close defense to basic wrestling and kickboxing moves. With the limits of the confined space and the lack of distractions, I practiced each day until I reached the point where I would be more lethal at a close encounter than long range.

I spent a lot of time visualizing fights, thrusts, blocks, attacks, and countering them until the motions became instinctive and my body reacted fluidly to every encounter I could imagine. My goal wasn't to kill, just to defend in a way that I could wear them out, protect myself, and hopefully make them look stupid in the process. I just hoped it was enough.

The guards came irregularly to pull me out to the blood room for beatings. The sensitivity my eyes formed to the light in the rooms outside my dark cell alarmed me, but I didn't know what to do to counterbalance it. That would have to be a bridge I crossed when I came to it. They took the cloth down from the camera the first few times they came into my cell, then gave up. I assumed they decided that whatever I was doing wasn't worth worrying over, and they would be rid of me soon enough.

Chapter Nineteen

The last beating was different. They avoided my head and wings and instead focused on my ribs and stomach until I felt the ribs give under their gauntleted knuckles and organs bruise until I worried that they wouldn't function correctly afterwards. When they finally released the chains that bound my wrists above my head, I fell to the floor in a daze of pain. I didn't realize until they dragged me into the cage that today was the Blood Match.

A guard grabbed my hair and yanked my head painfully back. "Now be sure to put on a good show. We don't want you dying without a fight." He gave a cruel laugh and spit on my face before releasing me. I crashed back to the cage floor and lay there trying to gather my strength. A few minutes later, guards entered the cage with the armor I would wear for the fight. They strapped it on while others held whips and spears ready in case I put up a struggle; then they backed away without a word and left me in the small, empty gray room in silence.

I fought back an ironic chuckle. The guards didn't even bother with the pretense that this fight was for honor. After our brief jaunt of freedom, we all knew the fights were for a television show. I couldn't decide if it was good or bad that the guards gave up the lie. I shook my head and tried to focus past the pain of my beating.

This was it. I didn't know what to expect up there, only that it would be different than any other Blood Match. Most states had gambling halls that had been legalized for the Arena battles. No doubt they were filled to the brim today.

I took several slow breaths to clear the fog from the throbbing pain of my broken ribs and aching stomach, then pushed myself to my feet to survey my armor in the hopes that the guards hadn't found yet another way to sabotage me.

The armor was light and looked more intimidating than it was functional. Deep etches outlined feathers in the light silver that barely covered my chest, ending at the bottom edge of my rib cage and leaving my stomach bare. Gauntlets ran from the middle of my forearm to my fingers, ending in clawed tips like eagle talons that would protect my fingers but left me free to use my sword.

The armor that covered my wings to the joint and my back was also etched with feathers burnished light and dark silver. The mask that had been fastened on fit well and didn't obscure my vision.

In all, the thin armor would do little more than protect me from glancing blows, but at least it was something. I had to give the Arena credit for making us look more like animals than humans, something definitely in their favor if they wished to continue the battles. An echo of my instructors' words from when I was young repeated in my head.

"The Arena is sacred. You fight for much more than honor, you fight for your place in the heavens. An honorable death is the only way to ensure that you live beyond the Arena walls. Do your duty to all of us and wear your mask with pride. The Arena sands are sacred; covering your face is a sign of respect for the honor you have been given."

The gong rang, tearing my thoughts back to the present and signaling the start of the match. The door to my cage opened, revealing a short, steep walk to a hatch that opened slowly, giving access to the Arena above. I gritted my teeth and pushed my pain to the back of my mind. There would be no time for weakness when I reached the square of light.

I rose slowly to the top and squinted in the suddenly bright light. It took a few seconds of precious time for my eyes to adjust to the light of the Arena. I crouched low expecting an attack, but was surprised when my vision cleared enough for me to make out David, Goliath, and another Galdoni I had sparred with a few times. I wasn't sure what he called himself. The Academy name VZ790 came to mind from our encounters.

Goliath and David hurried to my side.

"Kale! It's so good to see you! We thought you were dead!" David said excitedly.

I gave them a relieved smile even though it was hidden behind my mask. "I thought the same about you. Looks like we get to enjoy this together."

David's eyes creased with humor behind his mask at the sarcasm in my words, which surprised me. As my eyes adjusted, I got a better look at him. He appeared stronger, wirier. He walked with the lethal grace of a hunting cat instead of the gangly youth amble I remembered. "You've been training hard," I surmised.

He nodded. "Fighting to not fight," he whispered with a wink.

By this time, Goliath and the other Galdoni had reached us. Goliath looked me over. I stood casually in an effort to hide my bruises, but his brow furrowed. "You're not in any shape to fight."

I shrugged and shook out my wings, enjoying the added space. "Not like we have much choice, is there?"

A rare smile touched his eyes. "No, I guess not." He backed off a few paces into a defensive position, but I caught his bass chuckle as he settled himself.

"Where do you suppose they are?" David asked, only the slight tremor in his voice giving away his fear. His eyes, the only thing I could see behind a hunting cat mask, darted from side to side. I glanced in his armor and saw the reflection of

218

my own mask; I had to fight back a grim smile. A falcon's sleek head, smooth brow, and wickedly curved beak glittered in the light; with my armor, it looked especially intimidating.

I glanced around the Arena. "Don't know," I responded. I studied what I could see of the walls. The Arena had been overhauled. Pillars of stone rose in varying places around the floor, giving ample room for the other Galdoni to hide. The ground had been filled with hard sand that slowed our movements. It would be easier to fight in the air, which I assumed was the intention.

"Looks like they're trying something different," VZ790 said from my left. "We've never been in groups before, and weaponless."

I nodded to indicate the three of us. "They're trying to eliminate us as a threat. How about you?"

He stared at me, the astonishment of my bland statement bright in his eyes. "Are you ready to die then?"

I shook my head. "I'm ready to give them a fight they'll remember."

He studied the pillars around us for a moment, then nodded. "I stir up a little mutiny, I get thrown in here with the ringleader." He took a step back and offered me his hand. "I'm Varo. Nice to have the pleasure of creating trouble with you."

I laughed and shook his hand. "Kale, but I guess you already knew that."

He nodded and repositioned himself a few paces from my back. Goliath and David followed our lead. Each paced a few yards to our left so we could defend each other.

"Here they come," Goliath said.

My stomach soured. At least they could try to make it look like a fair fight to the viewers. Four Galdoni, led by one of Blade's closest followers, appeared on the pillars above us.

219

They held serrated swords that glittered in the Arena light. Each of the Galdoni wore dark blue armor and reptilian masks covered in lethal spikes along every edge, uniting them as a team.

"Weapons!" David shouted.

I glanced over and saw four short swords rise from the sand. "I'll get them," Varo said. He ran toward them and ducked just in time to avoid a diving attack from the Galdoni closest to him. Varo grabbed up the swords, blocked with one, and tossed the others in our direction.

I caught one out of the air and turned in time to parry an attack from the lead Galdoni. The other two followed close behind him, obviously under orders to finish me off before I could cause any trouble.

"Missed me?" I growled with a taunting grin at the first Galdoni.

His eyes widened and he lunged at me again, aiming for my heart. I parried his sword aside, rolled backward, and kicked the legs out from one of the other Galdoni. When he fell to his back, I jumped up and knocked him on the head with the hilt of my sword. He collapsed unconscious on the ground.

"Don't worry, he'll survive," I said as much to anger their leader as to update the viewers. I wondered if the Academy had time to cut that out before it was broadcasted, and fought back a triumphant smile. This was going to be fun, or at least as fun as a battle for one's life could be.

David ducked a Galdoni's sword, then Goliath picked the attacker up from behind and threw him into one of the pillars. The pillar broke with the force of his throw and crumbled to the ground. The Galdoni fell to the sand and groaned, curling up around what I guessed to be very broken ribs despite the armor.

"Not dead," Goliath grunted. He flashed me a mischievous look and turned away to find another attacker.

I parried the leader's next swing and stepped toward him. He countered my blow and thrust again. I slashed the blade aside and stepped closer. His eyes widened and he stumbled backward, his blade swinging wildly. I parried again and twisted my sword so the hilt caught the serrated edge of his blade and threw it.

"You should probably keep a tighter hold on that next time," I recommended. He looked around wildly for another weapon in time to see Varo efficiently dispatch the last Galdoni using a sleeper hold.

"Feeling outnumbered?" I asked in a false sweet tone.

He growled and was about to dive at me when a sound above us caught my attention. I glanced up. Eight more Galdoni warriors, this time armed to the teeth with swords, knives, and maces, glowered down at us from the pillars.

"Look out," I shouted to my companions. The Galdoni glided down, weapons out and ready to use.

Nine to four, that sounded more like the Academy seeking revenge. I searched for an advantage while the Galdoni I had been fighting rolled back and grabbed a pair of knives from one of the new attackers.

"To the air," I shouted. I pushed my wings down hard and rose above the stone pillars. The other three followed close behind, swords in hand. We flew to the top of the Arena dome. Air currents rose in a way that allowed us to glide and watch what was going on below.

"Now what?" Varo asked. Blood streamed down his mask from a gash along his hairline. He wiped the blood away in annoyed gesture.

"We keep it up. Eventually, they'll run out of Galdoni who'll fight us, then they'll have to send in the guards. I'm hoping the public will see through that."

Goliath nodded next to me. His mask was crooked and a bruise already swelled his left eye mostly shut.

A glance at David showed his red hair ruffled and dirt streaking his cat mask, but he was otherwise unharmed. He watched me expectantly. Below, the Galdoni were rising into the air in a tight battle formation.

"Well," I said with more enthusiasm than I felt, "Let's show them what we can do."

I folded my wings and dove.

Even though we were in the midst of a battle, I couldn't ignore the thrill of the air rushing past my face and ruffling through my feathers; my wings, held tight to my sides in the dive, felt stronger than ever. Adrenaline pumped through my veins as the battle fury filled me. I fought back a laugh and spun to the left to avoid a knife that flew through the air. I used my wings to propel back to the right and angle above the nine Galdoni. A glimmer of grim blood lust filled me when I recognized Blade in his tell-tale gold dragon armor, a sword in each hand.

I spun to the left just in time to avoid his swords, then held out my arms before I reached the two Galdoni below him. The power of my dive knocked the wind from them as I forced them to the ground. They didn't have time to get their wings out to slow our decent. I opened my own a second before we hit, and lifted off to watch them thud to the dirt. A quick fly over showed them to be moving, slowly, but still alive.

"Two more down, but not dead," I shouted to the sky. Distracted, I barely heard the rush of wind that warned of an attack from above. I wheeled to the right, but not before one of Blade's swords grazed my back just below my armor. A cry escaped my lips and I felt the blood begin to trickle down.

"We won't be so kind to you," Blade taunted as he passed.

He turned a few yards away and came back, but I was ready this time and parried the blow with my sword. I rolled to the left, losing some altitude and giving him a perceived advantage. He took the bait and dove at me, using his height to aim for my wings.

I closed them the second before his blade would have severed my left one. He turned, off balance. I opened my wings and closed them to gain momentum, then slammed into his chest with my shoulder. He let go of his swords with the force of the blow; they fell toward the ground. Blade held onto me, too close for me to use my own sword. I tried to push him off so I could open my wings, but his arms trapped them to my body.

We plummeted to the Arena floor. It was obvious he planned to do what I had done to the other Galdoni. In desperation, I dropped my sword and reached up, grabbing both of his wings at the joints before he could open them and escape. His eyes widened and I felt a brief surge of satisfaction at the surprise on his face.

I heaved around to the right just before we hit the ground. The force turned us enough so that we both hit the sand on our sides. The blow knocked us apart. I struggled to catch my breath. Pulling in a ragged gasp, I glanced around for a weapon, sure he would be doing the same.

There were two more Galdoni close by on the ground. I didn't think they were dead, but couldn't stop to be sure. Overhead, Goliath and Varo battled four attackers in ruthless, headlong rushes. I struggled to my feet and looked around for David.

223

The young red-head stood a few pillars away, his back to me as he grappled with an armed Galdoni. David blocked the Galdoni's downward slice and punched him in the ribs. He then grabbed his attacker's knife hand and tried to pry the weapon away.

At the sound of a footstep on sand behind me, I rolled to the left and came up in a fighting stance.

"Look sharp," Blade growled with a wicked taunt. He threw a knife at my chest and I dodged to the left. My foot slipped on the sand and I stumbled. A thud followed by sharp pain laced outward from my thigh. I glanced down at the knife hilt that protruded.

"Too slow," Blade mocked. He tossed up another knife and caught it by the tip. "Let's see if we can't hit the other one, too."

I dove under the knife. It passed millimeters from my ear before I bowled Blade over. He kicked out and sent me over his body and into a pillar. I stood up and shook my head to clear the haze from my eyes, but Blade was already in front of me. He picked me up bodily and tried to back me into the pillar again, but I head butted him in the nose while simultaneously driving my knee into his groin. He dropped to his knees, a hand on each injured area.

I spun behind him and caught him in a choke hold. I looked up in time to see David throw his attacker to the ground. He gave me a wild grin. The young Galdoni then turned to his opponent as he rose unsteadily from the ground. David did a fancy back kick that was more for show than effect. But his opponent ducked the kick. Before I could move, the Galdoni pulled a knife from his belt and drove it into David's back.

David's eyes met mine, his own wide with shock. "Kale?" he asked, his voice strangled. He fell to his knees.

"No!" The cry tore from my throat before I could even comprehend what had happened.

I shoved Blade to the side and ran to David. The young Galdoni sputtered and fell forward. I caught him before he could hit the ground. Blood trickled from the side of his mouth to the bottom of his mask. The Galdoni that had struck him picked up a sword from the ground. I spun so that I crouched over David protectively.

"Touch him and I kill you all," I growled; a feral rage lifted my lips in a snarl. I heard several Galdoni land on the pillars above, but nobody moved toward us.

David coughed and red-tinged foam bubbled at his lips. I pulled him up so that he rested on my knees, his head cradled in my arms. Warm blood flowed down his back to pool on the indifferent sand.

"I didn't want to kill him," he wheezed out.

"Shhh, don't talk. Save your strength," I told him gently. Inside, I tore myself apart. He wouldn't have gotten hurt if it wasn't for my stupid plan. He could have killed the Galdoni earlier instead of worrying about keeping him alive. I gritted my teeth and cursed myself, my plan, and everything that had led up to this moment.

Steps came to my side. Goliath crouched next to me. He sniffed and I looked over to see tears drip from under his mask. He reached out and touched David's shoulder. "You fought hard," he said softly.

David gave him a weak salute with a hand to his chest. "Brothers to the end," he forced out. He held up a fist.

Goliath tapped the knuckles with his own. "Brothers to the end," he said before his words choked off. He rose and turned away; a sob tore from his throat.

"You've got to hang in there, David. Don't give up on me now," I told him.

He gave me a weak thumbs-up, then his arm fell heavily to the ground. His head rolled back on my arm. I gritted my teeth and lifted my arm so that he looked at me. "No, not like this, David. You're gonna get out of here. Stay with me." I looked around wildly for help. The enemy Galdoni stood a respectful distance from us. Blade leaned against a pillar, his eyes unreadable. Varo knelt on the ground a few feet away, blood streaking the armor across his chest.

"Kale?"

I looked back down at David and leaned close to hear the soft words from his innocent lips.

"Do you know what I'll miss most?"

I shook my head, not trusting myself to speak.

"Flying." The word left his lips like a sigh. His eyes drifted from mine and stared into space.

"No, David," I commanded. When he didn't respond, I shook him. "David, come on. You're going to be okay." I had to force the words out as my throat tightened. "You have to be okay." I shook him again.

A hand touched my shoulder and I knocked it away.

"Kale, he's gone," Goliath's pain-filled voice said above me. It took a few minutes for the words to sink in, for the finality of their meaning to cut through my chaotic thoughts.

I lowered David to the sand. A blind, red rage filled my vision. I rose to my feet and tore out the knife Blade had sunk into my thigh. With a cry of agony, I used it to cut the bindings on my mask. Gasps escaped the Galdoni around me when I threw the mask to the ground.

"You kill the innocent for your lies," I shouted up at the Arena dome. "Are you happy now with your pocketbooks padded in blood money?" I turned to the Galdoni around me. "And you! Curse you for fighting for *their* pleasure. We are not animals, yet you persist in acting like blood-thirsty beasts

226

because *they* tell you to. You have a right to live your own lives, but you have to believe that you are better than how they see you."

I threw the knife at the pillar next to Blade; it sunk to the hilt in the red sandstone. The Galdoni around me had waited quietly in respect to David. Now, to my surprise, they dropped their weapons. One Galdoni pulled the knife from the pillar and used it to cut away his own mask. He then handed it to his companion, who did the same. The other Galdoni passed the knife around, dropping their masks to the ground beside mine. Only Blade met my eyes and turned his still-masked face away, his head held high.

When the last Galdoni had removed his mask, I held out my hand for the knife. I used it to gently cut the bindings on David's mask. I gripped the cooling metal in my hands for a moment, then hurled it with all my strength across the Arena.

"He is not an animal. None of us are animals!" I shouted up at the dome. "And none of us deserve to die like this." I tore off my armor and threw it after the mask.

A grating sound heralded armed guards that streamed from openings in the Arena floor. The Galdoni backed up at the sight of spears and whips. I crouched over David's body as the guards surrounded me, lowering their spears threateningly.

I wouldn't kill them, but I would do whatever I could to make them pay for David's life. I motioned with my left hand; a strange, fierce, primal joy filled me at the anticipation of the fight. I flexed my wings with a snap and grinned wildly. "Bring it."

The guards stepped closer. One on the left stabbed at my side.

I spun, narrowly avoiding the point, and pulled the handle with me so that the guard fell forward. I chopped him in the throat with my fist and he fell to the sand. I spun, spear held handle-out, and parried four more spears thrust my way. I knocked their points down and to the left, then brought the handle back with enough force to crack all four of them across the face. They staggered as I spun to the right.

The point of the spear cut into my left hand, but the pain focused my strength and I held it tighter. I ducked under one spear, then knocked away a second and cracked the holder on the nose with the butt of my spear. A blade tore through my shoulder and I turned. I tore the spear away from the guard, then drove the butt of my own into his stomach. He doubled over in pain. I elbowed him in the back and he fell to the ground.

Another spear cut across my back. I arched backward with agony as a second guard forced a spear into my side. I turned toward him, driving my spear down behind his ear. The sound of it connecting with his skull echoed against the pillars as he fell to the ground. Another stab in the thigh drove me to my knees. My spear was yanked from my hands.

"Stop!" a voice shouted. My mind reeled with the pain, trying to place the voice within the Academy.

Someone kicked me and I fell to the side. My hands found the head of a spear embedded in the sand. I grabbed it and rose in a crouch. Two guards stabbed at me and I knocked their spears away, but the effort and loss of blood caught up to me. I fell forward onto my hands and knees and coughed. The motion tore through my ribs with agony. I tasted blood.

"Drop your weapons," the voice commanded. "You're surrounded."

A movement caught my eye and I turned my head. Armed humans dressed in black dropped from the ceiling on ropes and streamed across the Arena floor. They pointed guns at the guards surrounding me. The leader met my gaze with a relieved expression, then his eyes widened. He opened his mouth to shout, but something cracked against the back of my skull. I fell forward into the sand. Ringing filled my ears as darkness stole my vision. I felt vaguely grateful for the relief to my light sensitive eyes.

Chapter Twenty

Urgent voices and sterile scents beat down on me. I opened my eyes to see blinding lights checker past. I shut them again and felt the rush of air as I was pushed down a hallway. Something beeped near my head. A plastic mask had been fitted over my mouth; my lungs burned as I fought to pull in enough oxygen. Someone held my hand. I forced my eyes open again, turning my head to avoid the blinding lights. Several forms hurried along each side of me. I tightened my hand. The person closest to me leaned down.

"Kale?"

My heart slowed at Brie's voice. I tried to talk, but couldn't get the words out. Tears blurred my clouded vision.

"Kale, can you hear me?" Her words sounded distant as though she shouted them across a huge, empty room. They echoed in my head as unconsciousness stole me away again.

***

It was harder to push through the dark this time. It clung to my hands and feet; fingers of shadow caressed my cheeks, urging me to stay in the comfortable unknown. Steady beeps sounded in the distance, reminding me of something I had to do. With regret, I pushed past the darkness and pulled myself toward the light.

Pain. Before I opened my eyes, pain tore through my chest and raced down my arms and legs, awakening every wound. It was a different kind of pain than I had ever experienced before. This pain was weakening, desperate, the kind of pain that forces the soul back to the blackness and rest beyond.

But I don't have a soul, I reminded myself grimly. The pain let up only slightly, but it was enough. I forced my eyes to open.

An oxygen tube had replaced the mask, and the cool air rushed against my nose. I breathed in shallowly, aware of the deeper pain of my ribs and side. I took a few breaths and tried to slow my heartbeat. It raced as though I had just finished a fight, and it took all of my concentration for a few minutes to bring it down to a more normal pace. The beeping slowed.

"Doctor, is everything okay?"

I looked toward the sound of Brie's voice. Tension seeped out of my body at the sight of her. She stood next to three white-jacketed people near machines in the corner. Two of them consulted the third who studied the machines.

"If he was human. . . ." The man shrugged, frustration and concern evident in his voice. "I just don't know."

"It'd be nice if we had access to the lab records," one of the others replied angrily. "They have no right to keep those from us, especially given the fact that we're trying to save *him*. Who knows what valuable information they could have?"

I tried to swallow, but my throat was dry. "Their records were a little biased," I managed to rasp out.

They all turned in surprise.

Brie ran to the side of the bed and fell to her knees. "Kale, we thought we lost you!"

I lifted a hand to touch her cheek and was alarmed at how hard it was to do even that. "I'm pretty hard to kill. You know that." I gave her a smile.

She smiled back and tears filled her eyes. "They took you to surgery for hours, and when you were back in your room your heart stopped. They had to use a defibrillator." She glanced back at the doctors who now stood behind her, their eyes on me.

I remembered the rush of pain from my chest and gave a slight nod. "Thank you. I felt that."

One of the doctors laughed at the dry sarcasm. "Better than dead."

I shrugged, then winced at the pain that knifed through my shoulders. "Let me know next time you try it."

He chuckled and turned back to the machines. "You shouldn't be here," he said. He tapped some numbers that didn't mean anything to me. "You lost so much blood that we had to give you a transfusion. Your friend Goliath donated the blood. He fought everyone else who offered."

I smiled at the thought of anyone trying to argue with the huge Galdoni. Then I remembered David. Regret filled me. It hadn't been enough.

Brie read my expression. "We couldn't get in any earlier. After showing the video, we were able to convince everyone."

"The video worked?" I asked, surprised.

She nodded and squeezed my hand. "Yes, the video worked. People were ready to tear down the gates before it was even over."

I nodded and swallowed dryly.

Brie noticed and took a cup with a straw from the nightstand. "Can he have water, Dr. Benson?"

The doctor nodded.

She gave me the straw and I drank until I heard air gurgle at the bottom.

"Wow, thirsty," she said.

We both smiled. Heaviness stole through my body and I fought to keep my eyes open.

"Doctor?" Brie asked.

"He needs to sleep," Dr. Benson replied. He put something in the IV. It ran with a cold sting into my arm. "He'll heal faster that way."

Brie squeezed my hand. I shook my head. "I don't want to sleep." I slurred the words.

"Don't worry," Brie whispered as my eyelids closed. "I'll be here when you wake up. I'm never leaving your side again."

***

True to her word, Brie was there. Nikko, Jayce, and Dr. Ray beamed down at me from behind her. I smiled uncomfortably at the attention. "Is it too late to pretend that it was all a dream?"

Dr. Ray smiled. "Yep. Now you'll have to face the tidal wave your heroics have caused."

I met Jayce's eyes. He gave a huge smile. "Were you surprised it worked?" I asked him.

He laughed. "Almost as much as you, I think. I ran in with the others at the gate, but those Galdoni were ready to tear us apart if we so much as laid a finger on you."

I glanced at Brie for an explanation.

"When Jayce and Nikko stormed the Academy, the Galdoni there rushed to the Arena. Jayce's group made it just before the other Galdoni broke through. Looks like they had their own plans to stop the fight." She grinned at Jayce. "You could say it was a battle for who got to help take you out of the Arena. It almost became violent."

Nikko chuckled. "Yeah, lucky for us you had that 'no fight' policy."

"It was more of a 'no kill' policy at the end there," I amended with a slight laugh. I shifted to find a more comfortable position. Pain knifed up my side. I winced and settled back against the pillows that kept my weight off my wings and the wounds down my back.

"Well, you managed to do a pretty good job of making your point," Dr. Ray said. He squeezed my hand. "Good to see you're okay."

Nikko looked me over critically. "I don't know if I would call this okay. You're still not in the clear yet."

Jayce gave his trademark grin. "I don't know if he was ever okay in the first place."

"Hey," I protested. "As I recall, it took you a while, but I finally broke you down."

He nodded. "Well, you'll have to get used to charming your way into the hearts of the people. You'll have a lot of that to do when you get out of here."

"Jayce," Brie said in a warning tone. She threw me a worried look.

"What?" I asked.

Brie glared at Jayce, then she sighed and turned back to me. "You're kind-of the press' golden boy for Galdoni rights now."

My eyebrows rose. "How'd that happen?"

Everyone turned to Nikko and his cheeks actually reddened. "I, uh. . . I might have changed the video a bit with that intention in mind."

"A bit," Brie scoffed.

Intrigued and a little concerned, I asked if I could see it, but the doctors were still worried about my heart rate and wouldn't let them bring in anything that might cause excitement. My friends refused to give any details and made me wait a few more days before the doctors pronounced me fit enough to see it.

Chapter Twenty-one

The video opened on the picture of the tiny Galdoni baby asleep in the white gloved hands of a lab tech. The wings looked delicate and perfect, but they weren't white like the first time I had seen the picture. The wings had been altered so they were the black-purple hue of a raven's feathers. Their simple beauty matched the angelic, innocent smile on the sleeping baby's face.

The pictures then rotated to the toddler learning to walk, the toddlers in the classroom, and the toddler about to be whipped. Music started slowly, rising at the picture of the whip in the air.

But then the video changed to the next scene, and the mood of the music shifted subtly, darker tones taking over the simple cadence of childlike innocence.

The scene showed the boy with the katana, wings lowered and a tear on his cheek as he stared down at the dying Galdoni boy at his feet. It, too, was different than the first time I had seen the image. Instead of tawny wings, the feathers had been changed to black, just as Nikko had done to the children in the slides before. The boy's hair had likewise been darkened. I wondered why until the video showed the next scene of the younger me fighting the other Galdoni. In that transition, it looked like I had been the one in all the pictures.

My heart slowed as several more images I hadn't seen flowed through, images that were really me. I wondered how long they had searched for them.

I watched the younger me in the training room twirling a blade above my head. In the next image, I knelt next to a small Galdoni with brown wings and showed him how to hold a blade larger than he was in a firm grip.

236

Next, it showed the closing of the Arena, winged forms silhouetted against the morning sun. None of them were me, but it didn't matter because no one else could tell.

There were a few pictures from high school that I hadn't known had been taken, me in my coat at the back of Dr. Ray's classroom talking to Brie and Jayce, a room full of students at Zach's place with me in the background throwing darts. I had to smile at that one because I realized the tip of my feathers were visible at the bottom of the coat when my arm was raised to throw the dart. There was a picture of Brie and I standing in the rain in the backyard. A lump formed in my throat. I glanced at Nikko.

He shrugged. "I thought it would come in handy," he said apologetically.

Then there was a video of three figures on top of the old city building. Two looked like they were talking, and the third stood a bit further from the edge. The video blurred a bit and moved slightly, but it still did the job. I watched the first figure turn and fall backward off the building; the second caught his hand and was pulled over with him.

Even though I had experienced it personally, my heart skipped a beat when the second figure grabbed tight to the first; a coat flew up discarded behind them, then black wings opened and caught the air a second before they hit the ground. They soared low over the crowd and the jumper was set down before the Galdoni crashed a few feet away. He rose gingerly, his eyes wide as though he had just realized what he had done. The crowd swarmed and he disappeared from view.

The screen went black and the music grew quieter. Words appeared, white on the black screen. Jayce's voice read them solemnly. "The life of a single Galdoni. Not a monster, not an animal, but a hero waiting for his chance to live. We've been taught to see them as inhuman, but we can't deny the humanity Kale has shown." The black image changed to one of the Arena, the gates gray, cold, and forbidden. "Help us stop the violence that goes on behind these walls. Refuse to watch the fights; don't gamble on lives that should be spent in the pursuit of happiness, our right and theirs. Don't let Kale die because you didn't take a stand."

The tape paused and Nikko turned to me, "We thought you'd want to see what occurred at the Arena after the video. They tried to cut it off, but Iggy found a way to keep the footage rolling so everyone saw what truly happened."

I nodded and watched the battle from multiple cameras at the top of the Arena. I heard us talk, make our battle plans, and watched us dive toward the attacking Galdoni. The battle felt longer than it had in real life. I saw Goliath, Varo, and David's sides of the fight, acts of heroism in saving Galdoni they could have slain.

My throat tightened when David was stabbed, but I couldn't look away. I heard us speak, and heard his last words again, the words that had echoed in my head through my fever dreams.

"You know what I'll miss most? Flying."

I swallowed hard to fight back tears, but shook my head when Nikko asked quietly if he should turn it off.

I watched myself curse the viewers and the Galdoni who stood around me, and saw the Galdoni drop their weapons and take off their masks, all except Blade, who turned his back. I followed my battle with the guards, a losing battle before it even started, but one I refused to give up.

I felt the bite of the spear in my hand and glanced down at the bandages around my left palm. The scratch of stitches tugged at the gauze. I felt the bite of each wound as I watched them occur, but I didn't regret fighting. I didn't regret any of my own pain.

The video changed to a view outside the Arena gates. If I hadn't seen it with my own eyes, I wouldn't have recognized the square beyond because it was filled to overflowing with protesters banging on the gates and trying to get in. A few minutes later, someone with a big black SWAT truck rammed them repeatedly until they bent and fell inward. The crowd rushed past the twisted metal and swarmed the Academy walls. Nikko turned off the video.

I forced a slight laugh. "Wow, if I didn't know that Galdoni better, I'd follow him, too."

The others laughed and Nikko put a hand on my shoulder. "Well, he's going to have a lot to do when he gets out of the hospital."

I met Brie's eyes. "I can't wait."

GALDONI

*** Keep an eye out for the second book in the Galdoni series projected to be released in Spring 2014

About the Author

Cheree Alsop is the mother of a beautiful, talented daughter and amazing twin sons who fill every day with joy and laughter. She is married to her best friend, Michael, the light of her life and her soulmate who shares her dreams and inspires her by reading the first drafts and adding depth to the stories. Cheree is currently working as an independent author and mother. She enjoys reading, riding her motorcycle on warm nights, and playing with her twins while planning her next book. She is also a bass player for their rock band, Alien Landslide.

Cheree and Michael live in Utah where they rock out, enjoy the outdoors, plan great adventures, and never stop dreaming.

Check out Cheree's other books at www.chereealsop.com

Printed in Poland
by Amazon Fulfillment
Poland Sp. z o.o., Wrocław

58457532R00137